ALL THE
SERPENTS
IN THE SKY

S. R. DREAMHOLDE

POSTBUN PRESS

NOTICE TO THE READER

The subject matter contained within this book includes torture (off page), character death (off page), corpses, children in danger, explicit sexual conduct, racism, sexism, unwanted flirtation, resentment, mistrust, opposing worldviews, crises of faith, conflicting loyalties, mutual compromise, magic, decisions made under the effects of sleep deprivation, and references to war, invasion, and occupation.

For Andrew Lovett, who encouraged us to imagine and then inhabit our best selves, and at whose table we first fell in love. How appropriate that, twenty years later, Kahldar and Selida should do the same.

The Welded Dawnlands
North to the Troll Lands
Wintersend Keep
Wyvernsvow Keep
The Royal Capital
The Tidelands
West to Mythical Alonia
Skyfawn Citadel
& Aluna's Grand Abbey
East to the Welded Provinces
Coralglass Keep
The Lands of the Tide and Dawn
Prepared by Lydris Magnus for his Knight Commander, 1140
South to the Thraxian Principalities

Selida Coralglass knew that the only way to keep a secret was never to think of it; to become a new person, untroubled by its existence.

Today, she was failing.

As Dulcis plowed up the sandy hill beneath her, Selida felt her heart glaze over with lead—heavy, poisonous, and maddening. When they reached the crest of the bluff, she eased back in the saddle. The peninsula unfurled before them, but nothing she saw lightened her mood. Beyond her mare's ears, leviathan cliffs of white fog veiled a jagged tongue of land. Wyvernsvow Keep crouched unevenly on the horizon, watching over sharp rocks and gray ocean: a structure as oppressive, tiresome, and thoroughly Dawnlander as the oppressive, tiresome men from afar who had built it.

"This war will not end until that ungainly monstrosity falls into the sea." Her Tidelander father had made his

prophecy on this very rise, twenty years ago. His caval-cade of exhausted knights had muttered in sullen agreement as they tramped towards the then-new castle, built like a sneer over the broken bones of what had once been the coast's grandest Temple of Aluna.

Ostensibly, they had come to negotiate a surrender. Young as she'd been at the time, even Selida knew that Lord Coralglass intended for Laurence, his son and heir, to continue the Tidelanders' war in due course. The parchment their father signed that day spoke of peace, but all he had truly desired was time: time to lick his wounds, time to rally his people, time for his children to take up his cause and finally drive the invaders back into their lofty, frozen mountains.

But the Dawnlanders had been smarter, their treaties patient, and the years corrosive to rebellion. Now Lord Coralglass was gone, and his lands belonged not to Laurence but an agent of the distant king he had despised. Selida had taken holy orders, burying the past in the beachwood box where it belonged. But each year, when Aluna's ministry took her to this haunted rise, her father's words returned like an echo embedded in the roar of the sea. Expectant. Waiting.

Each year, she ignored them.

An alarmed shout penetrated the fog. Grateful for the distraction, Selida brushed the familiar ghosts aside.

On the road below, a miserable knot of farmers and fishermen clustered around a cow which had collapsed among their carts. It bellowed with distress. The travellers, short-tempered with fatigue, tried to prod it back into motion with pitchforks and invectives.

Selida's neck prickled. The harvest had been short. Hunger was starting to spread, with banditry following close behind. This lane was ripe for an ambush.

She murmured a prayer, and the ocean-colored flags adorning the keep snapped into focus as Aluna's grace sharpened her vision. Steel helmets paced between crenellations. Both arbalests stood ready. The towering drawbridge denied entry.

Several children hidden in the snarl of wagons began to cry. Selida lowered her eyes to the hairpin turn ahead of the refugees.

There.

Brigands.

They wore patched leathers and carried rocks and cudgels. To her surprise, she saw more were crouched in the low brush all along the ragged column. *Why had they not yet attacked? Where was Wyvernsvow's escort?*

Then Selida saw him: a lone knight, previously obscured by boulders, guiding the front of the column up the switchback path. The grille of his helm covered his features, but her heartbeat knew him. His assurance. His grace. Even in the gray light, he gleamed, and his black warhorse bristled with weaponry. The knight's imposing presence had dissuaded the brigands thus far, but when he turned back down the path to investigate the delay, their mood changed.

Selida saw one raise a horn. The men hidden in the scrub drew axes and slings.

Well, we can't have that. Estimating distances and timing in her mind, she leaned forward and urged Dulcis into a gallop.

Kahldar only saw the ruffian in the tree when the man loosed a well-aimed stone at the graybeard minding the lead cart horse. When the fellow screamed and clutched his forehead, the beast shied, threatening to upend the vehicle behind. The road erupted into chaos.

"Backs to the wagons!" Kahldar bellowed to the farmers. He spun his mount Ispen to meet the foes as they closed in. "Guard the children!"

Extending his shield, he deflected another missile headed for a boy whose white-knuckled hands gripped a pitchfork. The lad yelped and swung wildly as he tried to defend his cowering siblings.

Counting at least twelve armed bandits, Kahldar kicked his steed into a knot of them before they could skewer a pair of shaking stablehands. Drawing steel, he forced the attackers away from the youths. Then he and Ispen plunged into the familiar rhythm of combat, moving as one without hesitation or conscious thought.

Exoeras damn that cursed Tidelander treasure.

If young Lord Lydris had not found the secret hoard of Elven gold in the caves under Wyvernsvow earlier in the year, these refugees would still be safely at work in their fields. Instead they risked death, both here on the road and in the soon-to-be-besieged castle they were bound for.

Mere hours ago he had warned the knight commander, "Tripling the guard at the keep until the King's taxmen arrive will leave any latecomers unprotected."

"You've seen the great hall—they're already stacked to the rafters," Ser Aegison had replied. "There's no room for more, and almost all of our serfs are already accounted for anyway."

"Indeed. Still, we are charged with protecting all of Lord Lydris's people, not *almost* all of them."

"Go, then, if you are so determined," Aegison scowled. "But with news of the Fox's army of murderous Tidelander knights and pirates growing daily, I will not spare one more man from the walls."

Now surrounded, Kahldar parried an axe swing and knocked another brigand back with the flat of his blade. Out of the corner of his eye, he saw three more bandits advancing on a woman defending a cartload of children in the rearmost wagon. With no way to close the distance in time, Kahldar shouted to draw the men's attention. Flipping his sword to his shield hand, he reached for one of the javelins holstered at Ispen's flank.

Before he could launch the weapon, a horse the color of surf materialized out of the fog at the back of the column. Astride it, sea-blue robes streaming behind her, crouched a lady cleric of Aluna... *that* lady cleric of Aluna. Buffeted by a whirlwind of memories—last year's festival

—the joust—that dangerous moment in the stables—Kahldar shifted his weight involuntarily, causing Ispen to step in her direction. Recognizing the futility of the impulse, Kahldar grit his teeth as the bandits swivelled their spears from the cart to meet her charge.

Instead of shying aside, the cleric rose in her stirrups, right hand flying skyward. As her horse gathered itself and launched them into the air, her voice rang forth: "Serpents of the earth!" she called, "Aluna bids thee answer!"

At the crest of the leap, the cleric threw her hand downwards.

With an explosive ripple, the wood of the brigands' weapons—every cudgel, spear, and axe haft—turned into angry snakes. Fat brown pythons, little black adders, and hooded, venomous cobras, all heaving coils of muscle, scales, and teeth.

The bandits screamed. Some tried to fling the beasts away from themselves, but to no avail: Fangs leapt straight for faces, striking noses, eyes, and mouths. Behind him, Kahldar heard the nearest ruffians fall to the ground, thrashing. The rest fled screaming into the scrub.

For a moment, the farmers simply stared, as disoriented as their attackers. Then they raised their makeshift weapons high.

"Praise Aluna! Tidemother!" Their cheers vibrated with full-throated relief.

The lady cleric bowed in her saddle and trotted her horse around the wagons. Kahldar halted Ispen at the top of the column and sought to compose himself. His breathing slowed, but his heartbeat stubbornly refused to steady. Watching her approach, he felt his own relief dissolve into a familiar—and far safer—irritation.

After accepting accolades from each farmer and fisherman, their savior paused her dancing horse before his. She was still grinning, cheeks flushed, eyes glittering. In her presence, Kahldar found it impossible to dismiss the far-fetched claims of ancient Elven ancestry woven into many a Tidelander ballad. Even more than Selida's elegant features, though, it was the exultation in every line of her body that riveted his gaze.

It had been a graver mistake than he'd thought, allowing himself to recall her face during those long, cold nights on guard duty. While it had eventually worn his memories of her temptress's smile translucent, that only left him more vulnerable, now, to the tidal-wave force of her vitality in the flesh.

"Ser Kahldar Whitepeak," she carolled. "Blessings of Aluna upon you. How are you enjoying this season's harvest of bandits?"

"Lady Selida. As fond of serpents as ever, I see."

Her grin flashed white. "Serpents lie at the root of all Aluna's creation and, to my joy, they never tire of my company. Unlike, perhaps, yourself?"

He drew a careful breath so that when he spoke he would not sound as churlish as he felt. "Excuse me. If you are done with your impetuous show of force, I must go ensure that your people do not now beat their assailants to death."

She shrugged, glancing to where the farmers were converging on the fallen bandits. "Both predictable and inefficient. As you like. I will mind the carts, and make sure these piglets do not run off while you enforce your Dawnlander justice."

As Kahldar turned away, he saw the tangle of snakes crowding the road slither up to her horse and stiffen obligingly back into cudgels.

Exoeras preserve me.

CHAPTER

TWO

Selida's people were not happy to be interrupted by their armored escort. As Kahldar positioned his steed between them and the now-cowering bandits, some of the farmers and fishermen looked to her for support. Reluctantly, Selida ignored their righteous indignation.

For twenty years, the treaty of Wyvernsvow had subjected the Tidelands to the Dawnland Dominion's rule of law in exchange for Aluna's continued sovereignty in matters of faith—at least in her traditional strongholds along the coast. Recently, though, Selida had felt the Dawnlanders circling closer, trying to wedge their wretched Welded religion in through the gaps in the inked words. To protect this next generation of Aluna's children, she dared give them no excuse to do so, even if that meant depriving these people of the blood debt that was their due.

With some effort, Kahldar persuaded the group's most strident member—the headwoman of a nearby village—back to her crying children. Selida dismounted beside her and offered her hands for a blessing. The woman, still red with outrage, accepted with a grudging bow, and the temperature of the entire group eased into an acceptable simmer.

By the time the caravan was all sorted out, Selida had taken the headwoman's two girls onto Dulcis's back, and only one of the bandits was in danger of expiring from the beating he'd suffered.

Kahldar remounted his horse. "Lady Selida, would you please grant this man the healing touch of your goddess?"

Selida looked down at the broken man, and then at her muttering people. Having cooperated thus far, she should not contradict him now. Still, she hesitated. "Are you sure? Aluna rations Her blessings as carefully as a sailor does her drinking water. If one of your men comes to ill tonight, you may wish I had saved the prayer for him instead."

Kahldar looked past her, towards the farmers and fishermen that tended Wyvernsvow's coast. "It is true that these men assaulted you, but, before these sad times, they were your neighbors. Lord Lydris alone has discretion over the fate of these criminals, and in this season of troubles he has judged it punishment enough to deny such miscreants the safety of his walls. Do not take any more of their blood upon your hands."

Selida saw many of her people look away, chastened. Dispensing justice and mercy from on high was not the Tidelander way, but it certainly made for excellent theater.

With a sigh, she passed Dulcis's reins to the older of the headwoman's girls and went to crouch beside the fallen man. His left leg lay at an unnatural angle, and bruises bloomed through his skin from cracked ribs and ruptured organs. Closing her eyes, she touched his forehead, and opened her other hand to accept Aluna's divinity. It surged down her palm and across her chest like a cool sea swell. At her next breath, it rushed out her fingertips with the hiss of foam on sand. She opened her eyes and watched the wave of power consume the body on the floor, flooding out the bruises and straightening the bone with a snap.

The man gasped as the pain receded.

"The Serpent of the Sea has closed your wounds and knit your bones," she intoned—once in Elven, then again in the trade tongue for those watching. "By the Tidemother's Law of Salvage, your life now belongs to Aluna. Live the rest of your days in Her name."

She wiped her hands on a towel she kept at her belt, and accepted the reins back from the wide-eyed children. The healed man's eyes followed her, flicked to Kahldar, and then lowered, downcast. As the caravan resumed its shuffling progress towards Wyvernsvow's lopsided bulk, the remaining bandits watched it go. Then, leaning one upon another, they limped back off into the fog.

Selida saw Kahldar's posture relax. As she counted heads and watched farmers corral their animals, he allowed his giant black horse to fall into step beside hers.

He opened the faceplate of his helmet. "I must ask: What brings you here? The harvest festival isn't for another three weeks."

No word of thanks? No courtly flirtation? Ah, Ser Kahldar. No wonder she'd spent the summer imagining new ways to make him blush.

Selida glanced back over her shoulder. Dulcis's passengers giggled to themselves as they pretended to be fine ladies. She lowered her voice anyway. "The Grand Cleric fears the roads will not be passable much longer." Tossing her stole over her shoulder, she smiled up at him. "So here I am."

He frowned. "How closely does your Grand Cleric still honor her oath to King Harald? Some believe the Fox has received arms from several coastal lords known for their devotion to your Tidemother."

Selida sighed. A Dawnlander might have been offended, but Aluna taught that the sea absorbed all blows. "Rumors." Before them, the caravan paused over some issue with a recalcitrant pig. "I ran to the Church to avoid these dramas. How was I to know it would not all be singing and dancing in the surf?"

Lamentably, he did not color at this comment. Surely he had not forgotten. She would never have accosted him in the stable had she not felt the heat of his gaze all through last year's Autumn Shoredance. Instead he replied: "Such rumors are no laughing matter. The King was willing to send a pair of his own Welded priests down from the Dawnlands to winter in Wyvernsvow. His advisors judged it safer than relying upon your aid. Ser Aegison wanted to accept."

She smirked to hide her grimace. "What lucky couple would that duty have fallen to? So far from their superiors, this priest and priestess might have escaped the strictures of their oh-so-holy arranged marriage." An extravagant sigh of mock regret. "Unfortunately for them, it would violate the treaty if any agent of the Welded Church were to preach in the Tidelands."

The Welded *W* on the rondel protecting the joint between his pauldron and breastplate winked at her, even in the diffuse light. "So Lady Magnus reminded him. She persuaded Ser Aegison to decline the offer."

"Thank Aluna for Emmeline."

He looked at her directly for the first time this afternoon. His golden eyes were sharp in a face more stern than its years. "So why are you here, Lady Cleric? Do you truly expect the people of Wyvernsvow to trust a woman whose Church is believed to have armed our soon-to-be-besiegers?"

It felt good to let her impatience show. Just a little. Just enough. Selida pointed to the caravan as a farmer's child got the sow moving again. "All these people belong to Aluna. They do not deserve to be caught between two eels, squabbling over a trout. I am here to ensure they survive the winter."

"And what are your feelings towards the Fox?"

She measured her words. "All the coast would be well served by a solution that spilled no blood, on either side."

"He's raised a host to claim a treasure that is the rightful property of the King."

"Then give them some of it."

His hand cut through the air. "Absurd. Social harmony, as well as common sense, forbids it."

"Then it is fortunate it is not you I must convince, but Emmeline."

"Lady Magnus knows the importance of Dawnland law and custom, even if you do not."

She sweetened her tone. "Then you have nothing to worry about from me."

He searched her face, as though it were a mask he could dissolve with a glower.

How exquisite. Selida scrutinized him in turn. Her gaze travelled from his dark brows to his fine lips, and then downwards.

He set his shoulders, but not before she saw his cheeks begin to flame. "Then make your petition. And when it is done, keep to your sacraments. I am pledged entirely to the keep's defense this winter. And even if I were not, my vows leave no room for your... flirtations."

Ah. Genuine pleasure crept into her smile. "Appallingly direct. And here I hoped you might have amended your vows, or at least be ready to apologize for where we left off last spring."

His tone flattened. "Why must you Tidelanders make every interaction fraught with blandishments?"

Her smile spread. "This conversation counts as blandishment?"

"Yes. You—*caress* your words with your mouth as you speak them."

Delight infused her. "Do women not practice flirtation in the Dawnlands?"

"No."

"Then how are they supposed to express *interest*?"

"They braid a wreath of winter wheat."

"What if it's not winter?"

"Then they wait."

She laughed. "What if he becomes otherwise engaged before then?"

His stare was yellow, and sharp. "Lady Cleric. Do not mock me. I am a knight of no land and no prospects. No liege waits to pay a bride gift on my behalf. Without such an exchange of goods to balance the deficit left in a woman's family when a man takes her to wife, Exoeras dictates that neither party has any business consorting."

Tidemother drown the Welded Church of the Heavens. She sighed. Pointedly.

Years ago, Selida had read the holy Welded texts acquired in secret by the Church of Aluna. They had not struck her as particularly inspired. A priestess of Era, Goddess of the Moon and Chaos, had begun a covert affair with a priest of Exos, God of the Sun and Order. As if playing out some lurid bard tale, their warring followers had murdered them and left their bodies in a single, shallow grave. By some grisly miracle, their dead flesh had then merged together to rise again as Exoeras, prophet and child of their two newly-reconciled gods.

Selida might have forgiven this gruesome faith's narrow sentimentality if the Welded did not also preach that all other gods, Aluna included, were mere aspects of their founder's divine parents, to be subsumed accordingly into their one great Church. She opened her mouth, considered, and closed it. The only thing more irksome than listening to Welded scripture was having her own religion explained to her by a Dawnlander.

Instead she offered: "So if I were a good Welded girl, you would expect me to hold my blandishments until your liege purchased me for you? Like a new suit of armor?" She glanced thoughtfully down at her torso, loose robes belted securely at the waist, and her booted feet, emerging from under split skirts. "Perhaps a horse?"

His cheeks reddened further. "Must you always make light? Exoeras' Law of Balance is far more sensible than pagan ceremonies like the Tidelander moon festival. Even in your own poetry it always ends in much wailing and rending of hair."

"How astute of you. And yet, that's part of its purpose. Without some wailing and wasting away, how is a young woman supposed to become wise enough to make her own decisions?"

"She would not need to curb her tendency to chaos if

she but allowed older and wiser people to make those decisions for her."

Selida tilted her head up to regard him with droll amusement. "I am older than you. By at least a few years, if I am not mistaken. Are you ready to submit to my greater wisdom?"

His warhorse jinked in her direction. "You are *not* older than I am."

Selida put her hand on Ispen's warm flank, inches from Kahldar's knee. "You can ask Lady Magnus, if you like. I carried the shells at her wedding."

She savored his incredulous silence as the road turned and the castle towered over them, gnashing turrets and black crenellations materializing through the fog. From this angle, she could not see the half of it that projected nonsensically far over the water, as if the castle's late architect had thought his task was to build the coast's most intimidating garderobe.

Almost there, but not yet. She inhaled the cool, wet air. *A few last moments of mist and white light, before a long winter of tiny, dark rooms.* She pushed even darker thoughts away. *Not yet.*

Kahldar leaned away, and Ispen stepped out of her reach. His voice was clipped. "I cannot, and do not, aspire to the sort of position that would allow me to offer you a dower arrangement. Without one to guarantee our material happiness, as well as peace between our families, your flirtations court disaster." He took a breath. "I find them unwelcome."

She made her voice indulgent. "The assumptions that underlie your logic are lamentably flawed."

"You would think so."

She ignored him. "First, Tidelanders may not make war on those within their families, lest the serpents of the sky rebel. The Church excommunicates those who do, rendering conflict between our families impossible. Second, we have our own dower arrangement: a gift from the bride's family to the bride herself." She slid him a glance. "When a cleric of Aluna deigns to marry, the Church holds monies from her holy works in trust for her children. Which would neatly assuage your concern about material happiness."

He opened his mouth but, before he could speak, the lead plow horse stopped at the edge of the ravine separating the road from the tip of the peninsula.

With an impatient glare, Kahldar snapped his attention away from her and raised his mailed gauntlet. The men on the ramparts over the gatehouse returned his salute before disappearing to work the drawbridge.

Up close, Wyvernsvow looked even more impenetrable than it had from the hill. She counted at least three dozen men on this shift alone. Ser Aegison's writ of conscription had hit the coast like a bad crate of fish, hollowing out many towns just before the harvest. Seeing this side of it, resplendent and faceless, made her stomach knot.

Kahldar spoke—relieving her, for one more moment, of the need to worry about tomorrow. "Do not bait me,

Lady Cleric. Any fool would judge a permanent union between us preposterously unwise."

At this she did laugh. "Oh! I agree." Her gaze softened. "But for other reasons than those you state."

His voice grew sterner, as if he and it borrowed the immovability of the castle before him. "Then this conversation is over. May I rely upon you to never raise it again?"

He genuinely looked as if he expected her to pledge her oath, right there on the road. She widened her eyes at him. "Ser Kahldar, not all flirtations must end in marriage."

His face set. "The Fox is coming. I cannot allow you to distract me this season." He kicked Ispen forward. "No good could possibly come of it."

Selida watched him go.

The smile faded off her face. He made her heart wistful in ways that were useless to examine. Instead, she coaxed the girls off Dulcis and returned them to their mother. Behind her, the tired line of people and wagons drained into the castle. Selida remounted and composed her expression. *Let the people of Wyvernsvow see nothing but Your will, Tidemother, as gentle and as inexorable as moonrise.*

CHAPTER

THREE

After settling Ispen in his stall, Kahldar paused at the top of the inner bailey stairs. Wyvernsvow's slate walls closed around him like a perfectly fit cuirass. He drew strength from its stillness. He could not allow his body's impious fascination with Lady Selida to persist. Long experience had taught him there was only one way to project the order his men and masters required of him: to become it, bone, blood, and sinew. *Thoughts, too. Thoughts most of all.*

Knight Commander Aegison stood outside the guardhouse door, frowning down at the chaos in the outer courtyard.

"Fifteen more refugees," Kahldar reported. "A combination of fishermen and farmers from a nearby town. I found them on the road about three hours away. Bandits trailed them. Nothing serious."

Ser Aegison was a Dawnlander like himself, but of an

older, harder generation. He stood with the leashed aggression of the mountains, silver streaking his black hair like snow. He had come to the Tidelands in the late Lord Lydris Magnus's retinue, and helped him win this swath of coast three decades ago. When Lord Magnus met his sudden end last fall, leaving behind his bride and whippet heir, King Harald had awarded the keep's stewardship to Ser Aegison in a letter signed by his own hand.

Now six years of age, young Lord Lydris Magnus was energetic and opinionated. He had discovered the treasure under the keep all by himself, in the early summer. Kahldar, who trained the boy daily, did not envy Ser Aegison the remaining twelve years to the lad's majority.

"And of these fifteen additional refugees, how many do you suppose secretly sympathize with the Fox?"

Kahldar said nothing.

Ser Aegison sighed. "Since you've found them, we will find room for them." The knight commander did not look up. Kahldar followed his gaze down to the figure in blue and teal robes swirling amidst the refugees. "Lady Selida Coralglass is early. Did she turn up with the bandits?"

Her name sizzled in his ears, but Kahldar was well practiced at holding his expression blank. "She helped us subdue them. She also healed their wounds and sent them on their way."

"*You* had her heal their wounds."

"We are here to cultivate the Tidelands. Those men may yet redeem themselves."

Ser Aegison snorted. "More likely they will run to the

Fox, and we will have to cut them down again when they march on this castle."

"Can the Fox turn a peasant into a fighting man in a matter of weeks? And even if the tall tales about him prove true, a phantasm must still feed those he recruits."

Ser Aegison's shoulders had almost relaxed when Selida's cheerful voice, echoing up from the courtyard, folded the knight commander's face back into a grimace.

"We'll need to keep that cleric of Aluna on a short leash. Those snake-worshipping lunatics are in bed with the lords of the coast, mark my words. They'd be just as happy to steal our King's treasure as they are to lure good men to ruin in the sea."

A memory stirred, unbidden, from the autumn past: Kahldar stood spellbound as Lady Selida led the devotees of Aluna in the old Elven shoredances. The harvest moon turned the sand to liquid gold. Her robes flattered her figure as they clung to her, translucent in the spray.

He dragged his thoughts back to the present. "She says her duty is the same as ours: to protect the people."

"Does she, now." Ser Aegison frowned. "She has a funny way of showing it. You had to haul her away from that flogging last winter."

He had. She had fought Kahldar all the way to the great hall. It was how he had learned, to his ongoing chagrin, that under her robes she was both sleek with muscle and generous in her femininity.

"As our late Lord Magnus explained it to me, Exoeras rest his soul, many Tidelanders still feel that such punishments are high-handed." Kahldar thought of the savagery with which the refugees had turned upon the bandits earlier. "They are more accustomed to rough, participatory justice."

"Adherence to—or defense of—those old ways is punishable by ten stripes."

Kahldar kept his face carefully wooden. "If you strike their cleric before their eyes, they will riot."

Ser Aegison swore under his breath. "Well, we'll have them all sorted out in a decade or two. For now, Lady Magnus clings to her pagan faith, or I would send Lady Coralglass on her way again."

"On what grounds?"

"At the very least, she's an agent of that medusa in the Grand Abbey. Worse, she's blood of Valerian Coralglass. Ten years and more in his grave, and that bastard's dishonorable tactics still plague my nightmares."

In the courtyard below, a pack of squires coalesced around Selida where she tended to her horse. Kahldar recognized them: the fresh cohort that had come down from the Dawnlands this spring. Selida returned their raucous greetings with unperturbed grace.

Kahldar forcibly pulled his attention back to what Ser Aegison was saying: "—Lady Magnus *claims* Lord Coralglass disowned his daughter before he died, but only Exoeras knows the truth of it. You are to assume she is up to no good."

Watching one of the squires in the courtyard sidle up to Selida, Kahldar tensed. Egged on by his peers, the lad offered a lewd proposition. When she coolly deflected and turned aside, he reached for the floating hem of Selida's stole. She snapped it away with a smile. Another young man reached for her backside. The refugees milling around the stable area went silent, watching.

Kahldar turned towards the stairs, but Ser Aegison's hand descended on his shoulder, stopping him.

As he was drawing breath to object, Selida flowed left of the squire, pivoted on her heel, and used the force of her entire body to slam him face-first into the stable wall. Kahldar heard the *crack* of his nose breaking from across the courtyard.

The pack of young men froze. The refugees in the vicinity settled back, content. Selida's smile did not waver, and her voice carried clearly: "Gentlemen. Aluna may smile on passion, but a serpent will still scar the hand that grabs its tail."

"She does not need your help," Ser Aegison said dryly, releasing Kahldar's shoulder. "Quite the opposite. These briny medusae are all teeth. If you wish to advance to my station someday, you must watch her, my friend—and watch yourself as well."

"Aye, Ser." Kahldar gave a short bow. "Your pardon. Some of our squires seem to have forgotten their vows. I must remind them, and then see to the young lord's training."

"I s this all the flour you were able to gather?" Selida finished her prayer and scowled at the larder shelves. Most years, the caves under the keep were packed with sacks of grain and barrels of fermenting vegetables. Gourds and hardy imported fruit usually overflowed from crates and boxes, while dried fish and kelp hung so thick from the ceiling that she would have to bend double to pass.

This year, the stores were so meager that Selida could already see the walls peeking out from between them.

Aluna damn the conscription, and double damn the short harvest.

Her prayers invoking the Tidemother's plenty had rounded out the bags a little, but nowhere near enough. With the extra burden of the farmers and fishermen sheltering behind Wyvernsvow's walls... she did the arithmetic in her head, and tried to ignore the sick feeling that slithered into her stomach.

"I'm afraid so, Lady Cleric." Dame Pottage, Wyvernsvow's head cook, lowered her voice so her words would be drowned out by the enthusiastic cheers from the keep's bailey. "We're going through 'bout a stone a day." She narrowed her eyes. "I don't suppose you might have some holy insight as to when the siege might start? Or maybe even... break?"

Selida did not flinch. *The only way to keep a secret is to forget it even exists.* "When these two sides see reason."

Dame Pottage's lips drooped sourly. "So we'll be in for a thin winter, then."

Selida waited for the sounds from the courtyard to abate. Moments after she'd broken the young squire's nose, Ser Kahldar had materialized in the stable. Looking past her as if ignoring her would erase her existence, he dragooned all the squires into an impromptu, grueling public training session.

"It's been at least an hour of this ruckus," Selida said. She resisted the urge to rub her forehead. "Are these displays... common?"

Dame Pottage selected a round of cheese to haul back to the kitchen. "Aye, Lady Cleric, and thank Aluna for Ser Kahldar's watchful eye. Misunderstandings arise every year when the young mountain boys first witness our rituals, but having everyone packed in so tight right now makes it worse. He's been keeping the freshest miscreants on notice."

She paused as another cheer burst from the crowd outside, and Selida caught a brief glint of mischief in the older woman's eyes. "If you ask the local girls, he's maybe a little too zealous in standing guard over such matters. They haven't had any more luck with him than you did, last year." She sighed, and tilted her head up the stairs. "Based on how it's going, whatever caused this latest bout offended his sensibilities something terrible."

Selida could watch Kahldar's spare, graceful style indefinitely, but she had not seen Lady Emmeline Magnus or her son in the courtyard. Usually, the chatelaine was the first to greet her people. Selida had stopped in the warm, herb-hung kitchen for some clue to this mystery, and found Dame Pottage fretting as she summed up mouths and the long months ahead of them.

Now, as she followed the spare woman back up from the larder, a crack between the mortared kitchen wall and the cave surface caught Selida's eye. Mouse droppings dotted the floor beside it. *That won't do.*

She reached into a belt pouch and pinched the bit of clay she kept there. Murmuring under her breath, Selida prayed a small portion of the rock nearby into a wriggling garter snake. It slithered towards the little black crack and forced itself into the gap before fusing back into solid stone.

Watching this, Dame Pottage kissed the shell she wore around her neck and nodded to Selida in thanks. . Hefting the cheese once more, she led the way to her workspace in the stew- and bread-scented room. "So you've glimpsed 'em all now, and done the counting your-self. Even with your prayers calling down Aluna's generosity, do you see why I've been so worried?"

"I echo your concern. I'm afraid—"

"Lady Selida, Lady Selida, welcome to Wyvernsvow!"

Ah. There they are. Selida turned from the busy hearth towards the high, clear voice. A bright-eyed boy—*Already so tall!*—with his mother's golden hair and his father's acorn eyes stood at the top of the kitchen stairs. He reminded Selida of a seal pup, though she would never say so to his face. A porcelain-skinned lady drifted in his wake.

"My Lord Lydris, my Lady Magnus." Selida curtseyed.

"But one moment." She turned back to Dame Pottage. "I agree that there is not enough in the larders to support this population through the winter. I'll continue augmenting our stores, but my prayers can only extend the supplies so far. You must enforce three-quarters rations, or we will run short of bread by midwinter."

Dame Pottage threw a glance at Lady Magnus. "Ser Aegison won't like that, milady. How can his men fight hungry?"

"I will speak with him," Lady Magnus said.

Dame Pottage curtseyed. "As you say, milady. And Lady Cleric. Thank ye kindly for your aid."

Selida turned back to young Lord Lydris, who was dancing from one foot to the other. "Yes, my lord?"

The boy seized her hands in his chubby paws. Swordsmanship calluses had just begun to cross his soft skin. In fact, instead of his usual teal tabard, he wore a too-large padded gambeson, with a practice sword stabbed through his belt. "Ser Kahldar says you routed the bandits by turning all their weapons into snakes. Do you still have them? May I see?"

"I heard you found a treasure under the castle," Selida countered. "Do you still have it? May I see?"

He scowled guilelessly up at her. "Nobody is to see it anymore, not even me. It belongs to the King."

"And I'm afraid those serpents belong to Aluna, and have returned to Her already."

His face fell.

She tapped one knuckle on the wooden table. "Serpents sleep inside all things, Lord Lydris, and they show themselves in our times of need. Perhaps another day."

"Lydris," his mother said, "I must show Lady Selida to her quarters. You must attend your practice. Ser Kahldar will see you out to the bailey and help you wash up afterwards. You may see Lady Selida again in the great hall."

Selida glanced up. The cheers outside had abated, and Kahldar now stood in the doorway, eyes fixed on something in the middle distance just past her shoulder. Stripped of his plate, complexion vivid and mud-spattered, he still filled the hallway, somehow even more substantial than he had been on the road two hours before.

"I don't need help washing," Lydris groused.

Kahldar's voice came, even and unruffled: "All of the pages clean up between practice and dinner. If you need no help, we will walk together to their barracks, and you may join them in their ablutions."

Lydris turned back to Selida. "Then you must sit at the high table with Mother and myself," he said, managing a charming impression of his father's former imperiousness. "We are anxious to hear news from abroad."

Selida's eyes widened helplessly as she met Lady Emmeline Magnus's black-veiled gaze.

"Time to go, my love," Emmeline said. Her voice was tired, but Selida could hear the pride in it, propping up the words like an animating force. The lady turned her son towards the door, but hesitated a long second before releasing him.

"He's grown terrifyingly fast," Selida said, as footsteps—one set measured, the other hectic—disappeared down the corridor.

"And I hardly know whether to push him forward or hold him back," Emmeline mused. "But enough of that." She turned, and her famously beautiful face folded into a gracious smile, familiar as a five-summer saddle. Even so, Selida could see that it was not only the black veil which rendered Wyvernsvow's mistress a wan shadow beside her glowing, golden son. Lady Magnus's grief seemed to have calcified during her year of mourning, settling into her bones instead of dissolving under tide and time.

Emmeline shook her head to forestall the unspoken questions she read on Selida's face. "Come. I have a surprise for you."

Selida, taken aback, let her friend loop an arm around her elbow and point them both towards the door.

FOUR

Selida had forgotten how glacial Emmeline's pace had become, her boned kirtle of black wool weighted down by jet-beaded overskirts and floor-length, sable-lined sleeves. Her memory of the Tide-lander princess who had once swum her by the hand through the royal kelp grotto trailed them up the coiled staircase like a ghost. The tower felt a hundred stories tall.

"I am sorry I was not in the courtyard to greet you, but from the window I saw Ser Kahldar's face as he left your side." Emmeline squeezed Selida's arm. "Do you plan to continue your pursuit?"

There were many things Selida wanted to discuss with Emmeline, but Ser Kahldar was not among them. She picked a neutral tone. "He might make for a fine splash in the surf, but I judge him far too prejudiced for anything more."

Emmeline continued up the stairs, past the family apartments on the second floor. "Ser Kahldar is a better study of Tidelander customs than Ser Aegison, and he has only been at Wyvernsvow since the spring before last. Perhaps his reserve will continue to erode with time and exposure."

"Ser Kahldar wants no further intimacies from me."

"Truly? Is that why he rebuked our young squires so vigorously?"

"Despite his overtures at the joust following last year's Autumn Shoredance, he made his position perfectly clear over the winter that followed. And again just this afternoon, in fact."

"And when has that ever stopped a cleric of Aluna?" Emmeline patted her arm. "Dawnlanders of his character are not the splashing sort. Their chastity thaws only with marriage." Pausing at the third floor landing, she tugged Selida into the narrow hallway. Beyond the arrowslit windows, the gray fog deepened into indigo. "You've made your dower contribution to the Church several times over, our Grand Cleric writes me. It would ease her heart to know you did not continue to gallivant up and down the coast alone."

"I am sure she would not want me to pick a Welded Dawnlander."

"Perhaps not," Emmeline said placidly, "but we must look to the future."

Selida swallowed her first reply. Before she could

shape a second, Emmeline stopped outside a small door at the end of the hallway. It was painted blue, and stencilled at heart-level sat the moon and sinuous waves of Aluna's faithful.

"Here we are," Emmeline said. "Your surprise." She reached into her sleeve and withdrew a brass key. "Go ahead. Open it."

Selida's lips parted, touched in spite of herself. She took the key, opened the door, and huffed a laugh.

"Do you remember it?"

Selida's fingers tightened on the key. "It was a linen closet. The year we all came to Wyvernsvow for the peace talks, you, Laurence, and I would hide up here to play. Our fathers could not bear the sight of us, after the discussions started to go sour."

Emmeline nodded, smiling. "I met Lydris here. He had come to investigate our scuffling. I knew at once that a man who could build this keep would build an equally solid alliance." Her voice softened further. "I stood on this spot and swore to myself that if our fathers could not make peace through words, then I would secure it with a wedding."

When Princess Emmeline Skyfawn had ended the war by marrying Lord Lydris Magnus, many people, including Selida's father, had far cruder words for what had happened.

Selida looked around. The little room now housed a dozen chairs, arranged in two half-circles. They faced an altar of wood, chased with mother-of-pearl. Behind the altar, two latticed windows looked out over the inky coastline. On the dark-blue-painted ceiling, winged and coiled constellations of white and gold circled the full moon. Under her boots, the floor undulated with teal dyes in patterns of snakes, waves, and tides. To her left, a banked fire smouldered in the hearth. To her right, an alcove housed a clean pallet and a beachwood trunk: open, empty, and waiting for her things.

With effort, she banished the fantasy of Kahldar, his dark hair tumbled across that clean bedding, from her mind. "It reminds me of your mother's chapel, in the old capital," Selida said instead. "And I am grateful for any private space, given your many guests." She considered her next words. "Did you fix upon it before or after the Dominion offered to send you an ordained Welded couple this winter?"

"Ah, you heard." Emmeline waved her hand in languid dismissal. "I've been mulling over this project for years. Lydris and I worked on it all summer. Of course, it is a poor replacement for the temple that used to stand on this promontory, but this is not the year to build a new church, no matter what your aunt writes me."

Selida bit her lip. "The Grand Cleric is merely concerned."

Emmeline tilted her head. "What, that the Welded will consume every religion in the Dominion?"

"That King Harald, upon his deathbed, will demand

every Dominion state convert to the Church of the Heavens."

Emmeline lowered herself onto one of the chairs, like a great bird folding in its wings for sleep. "Our treaty would doubtless preempt such a mandate. That said, I confess my heart has softened towards their scripture."

Selida unclenched her hands. "Do not tell me you would see the Dawnlands' sun god raised up as Aluna's equal, or allow them to claim She is merely some lesser aspect of their wifely goddess."

"I know. But surely you see that the Tidelands would be stronger standing together with the Dawnlands than apart."

"Hardly, especially if it requires us to be shackled to that Church. You cannot truly believe that every priestess of Era must wed a priest of Exos, lest the world fall into chaos."

"And you are in no hurry to pursue holy marriage and all it entails?" Emmeline smiled and closed her eyes. "Worry not. King Harald is decades yet from his grave. Aluna's rule over Her shores is as absolute as any mortal could desire."

Selida wanted to throw one of the wooden chairs out a latticed window. Instead, she crossed to the altar and began to set out candles and incense. "Luckily, no sane person would ever think I would make a suitable Welded wife."

Emmeline shrugged. "At dinner we will tell your petitioners where they can find you. Now, if you will light the votives, I would offer Aluna my evening prayers."

Darkness blanketed the coast outside, and the smoking sandalwood saturated the chapel. As the scent drenched her, Selida opened her heart. An old hymn came quiet to her lips, and she sang Emmeline's meditations into the black waters beyond. The familiar verses lent her quiet courage. In truth, she'd arrived three weeks early to pose a question to an old friend.

Tidemother, let us still be friends, after.

"*Have* you considered marriage?" Her devotions completed, Emmeline's voice floated dreamlike between them. "After the treaty, I remember your father had arranged a marriage for you—to a Dawnlander, like my Lydris. It is a pity that the Church chose that summer to requisition you from your family."

Selida hummed the last few bars of the verse. "Only a very special kind of man would be content to trail me up and down the coast."

"What if you petitioned the Grand Cleric to let you stay the year in Wyvernsvow?" Emmeline cocked her head. "You are not too old to try for children. You might still find that happiness."

I would rather eat glass. Selida turned towards the altar so Emmeline could not see her expression. She wondered if the prayers her charge had just offered up were for her living son, or the three she'd lost stillborn before him. Her marriage may have ended the war twenty years ago, but the peace it had bought now depended entirely on six-year-old Lydris. Selida took a deep breath.

"Lydris grows in promise with every passing day, but I can see that the events of this summer have worn on you." She found a seat at Emmeline's side, reached out, and clasped her friend's hand. "I am sorry."

Emmeline's eyes dropped to her lap. "Lydris and his father used to go to the caves together, every day. After my love's death, I could not deny him this one childish joy, so long as he took either Ser Kahldar or Ser Aegison with him." She shivered as she sighed, and Selida remembered the night before the wedding: the abduction, the frantic search for the bride-to-be, the rising water. Emmeline avoided the caves still. "And that was how he found this treasure. Sometimes I wonder if the villagers are right, and there is a curse upon it."

"So it exists?"

"Alas."

"I heard a rumor that the hoard contains an enchanted pearl, the sort our ancestors used to communicate across great distances. Have you seen such a thing?"

"Oh, as soon as we realized what we had, Ser Aegison declared the caves off limits. He fears a thorough accounting will lure good folks astray." The rings on Emmeline's free hand glittered. "I'm sure my husband would have done the same. Best to let the King's artificers handle the lot of it."

Selida hesitated. "I know you preserve his memory...

but it seems wrong to me to send it all to a foreign king. These treasures belong to our people."

"*Our* people? As opposed to *their* people?" Emmeline offered Selida the tiniest shake of her head. "I know it might be hard for one such as you to believe, but when I look at my son, I see that we are all one people now. If you were to bear such a child yourself, you would, I am sure, come to see it as I do."

One such as you? Undaunted, Selida plowed onwards. "Nonetheless, in Aluna's name, I would see this treasure with my own eyes. What if it rightfully belongs to Her Church? What the King has never seen, he will never miss."

"That is exactly the sort of temptation Ser Aegison seeks to avoid." Emmeline clicked her tongue. "Say no more, Selida. As much as I delight in your company, I will have no whisper of insurgency sully the future my son embodies."

Selida flexed her cold fingers. "I wish the Fox and his men could be so easily convinced. They see that hoard as their heritage."

"They disrespect the peace Lydris and I forged with our bodies and our blood. I have very little sympathy for their yearnings, backwards looking as they are."

This was it. Selida felt her breath, heavy in her gut. "All the same, if you or your son were... harmed by them, a whisper of insurgency would be the least of our people's problems."

A rekindling of war, was how the Grand Cleric had put

it, when she had called Selida to her office. *Fire that only blood will quench.*

Emmeline tried to tug her hand free. "Oh Selida, do not speak of such things, I beg you. Lydris and I know full well the burden he carries."

"And that *you* carry, seeing him to his majority." Selida ducked her head, trying to find Emmeline's green eyes under the shadow of her veil. "He is, what, six? Twelve years is a long time to persuade your neighbors to wait. And if he should fall ill—"

Emmeline did not flinch. "He is a strong boy. And he will be a strong man."

And now we are at the heart of it. "All of that is true, but you and I both know that *you* could be stronger."

A terrible silence. And then: "You are mistaken. Whatever it is you mean to say, stay your tongue."

Selida lowered her voice. "Emmeline, your marriage forced the coastal lords to stand down. Your blood ended the war, and it is your blood that now holds the peace."

Emmeline turned her face away.

Selida pressed on anyway. "Hold Wyvernsvow in your own name: as Princess Emmeline Skyfawn. Do this, and the Fox will either disperse his men or stand with you outright, should King Harald object."

Silence.

Selida squeezed Emmeline's fingers harder, because now both their hands were clammy. "You're tired, I know. It is not fair to ask this of you. But Lydris is young and the harvest was short. The winter storms may slow the

Dominion's reinforcements. I've seen the larders. Wyvernsvow will not survive an extended siege."

Emmeline barely breathed.

Selida reached into her quiver and drew her last arrow. "Emmeline, please. Don't let the people we once called kin slay those you now consider family. That is what will happen, if you and I do nothing."

Emmeline pressed her lips together. Selida could see her thoughts, flickering under layers of grief and exhaustion. Then she composed herself, pulling her spine upright. Hope rose. And then—

And then Emmeline cupped Selida's face with her free hand. Her voice was kind, but girded in iron. "Listen," she said, "because I will only say this once. If I do as you advise, the Dominion will crush us. King Harald will take my son away, destroy my husband's legacy, and render all my sacrifice in vain."

"Emmeline—"

"No." Soft. Absolute. "We must wait until Lydris attains his majority. If that means withstanding a siege by some faithless bandits, then so be it. The walls my husband built will stand."

Selida studied Emmeline's face, and found no chink in her wall of certitude. Her heart sank. She had taken enough confessions, and seen enough mothers, to know that she had made her gamble, and lost.

Fire that only blood will quench.

But there was nothing for it. She found her voice. "Alright, Emmeline. If this is the only way you see forward, I will not weaken you by making you doubt yourself."

Emmeline's breath escaped in a soft, pained laugh. "You could not take more than what Aluna has already taken from me." She released Selida's cheek. Her voice softened, regretfully. "I suppose you must now ride back to the Grand Cleric, to tell her of my refusal to cooperate?"

Selida stared at her. "What? That's madness. The Fox is nearly at your door."

"I doubt he poses any threat to you."

Selida's mouth fell open. She had underestimated her friend. She had walked into a trap, indistinct and courtly, made of words and compliments. The safest route out was to avoid—retreat-concede—but then she thought of all those people crowding the great hall. She thought of Kahldar, braced under the wall at Ser Aegison's command. "My lady," Selida tried, "without a cleric to heal the wounded and fill the cistern, Wyvernsvow will fall for certain."

"Is this the Grand Cleric's logic?" Emmeline mused. "She put you up to this, did she not? Is she so afraid of the Welded that she thinks to use you to persuade me to eat of poisoned fruit?"

"My lady, I don't—"

"Selida, as much as I would miss you, it would be safer for Wyvernsvow to have no cleric at all, than one who threatens the entire region with the taint of sedition."

"My lady, I came to aid the people of the coast. They need me as much as you do."

"If you go now, I will tell your parishioners that you were called away. They will not think you abandoned them in their hour of need."

"Emmeline, I cannot leave. I will not."

Lady Magnus shook her head, as if Selida were still half her age and slow to understand how the tides pulled at the millions of creatures that lived and danced within them. "I don't want to *command* you to go, of course. But how can I trust your advice will be in Lydris's best interests if your first inclination is to risk him in a bid against the Dawnlanders?"

"My lady, I want nothing more than for Lydris to inherit this castle, from you, in his time."

Emmeline ignored her. "And then there is your own standing to think of. If you stayed with me, even after failing to persuade me towards treason, would that not endanger your own position with your Church? I would never want that for you."

"Now *you* are presuming—"

"No, best to return to the Grand Cleric and tell her to send another woman in your stead next spring. That should signal that she ought not to meddle in Wyvernsvow's affairs. And through you, of all people! It is cruel and beneath her." Emmeline smiled wanly. "At least departing now will spare you a tiresome and hungry winter."

Selida heard the door of the trap close. She gave it one

second's serious thought anyway: imagined fetching Dulcis and sneaking out of the keep by the postern gate. She could go in the middle of the night, no one the wiser. *She sent me away*, she imagined saying to the Grand Cleric. *Wyvernsvow is in Aluna's hands now.* She imagined Kahldar, walking the halls, wondering why she had abandoned her people.

No. This is failure, but not yet disaster. As long as I breathe and reason, I can yet seek a bloodless solution. And if not... She dared not think of it.

Calling on all her self control, Selida steadied her hands, throat, and heart. With perfect, courtly correctness, she came to her feet and sank into a curtsey due a Tidelander princess. "Forgive me, my lady." Her mouth twisted, but she managed the words anyway. "I have misunderstood the situation, and it is only by the grace of your wisdom that we retain a path forward. If you would suffer my presence, I will do my utmost to aid our people through whatever siege may come."

Emmeline let her hold the curtsey at its lowest point as she considered this for ten long seconds. Finally, as Selida's thighs began to burn, Emmeline reached forward to help her back to her feet. "Then you will no longer speak of holding this castle in any but my Lydris's name?"

"I will not."

"And you are mine to command, for the duration of your time in Wyvernsvow?"

"As I always am, my lady."

"I am so glad." Emmeline sat back in her chair. All the

animation drained out of her, leaving her nearly transparent. Her voice was the whisper of a lonely ghost. "I would have missed you terribly."

Selida stared at the floor as Emmeline slowly rose to her feet, gathered her fabrics to herself, and drifted to the door. Step after step after step. At the threshold, she paused, and Selida heard the sad smile in her voice: "Really, Selida, whenever I thought of you over the summer, it was to wish you the happiness now forever lost to me. So if you are truly mine to command, I command you: Consider Ser Kahldar seriously."

This? Now? Selida contemplated not taking the olive branch, imagined letting her pride carry her to the altar where she would drown out this conversation in another litany from Aluna's scripture. *War, starvation, or worse,* she reminded herself. Her pride would have to swallow seawater. It wouldn't be the first time.

"Because you wish it, I will keep that in mind," Selida managed.

"You know, the guardsmen now maintain an evening rotation," Emmeline added. "They're up on those parapets all night, watching for the Fox and his men to show themselves. Ser Aegison does not want them distracted, but some tea would help them stay awake. You might take it upon yourself to bring it to them."

"I am sure Ser Aegison would regard that as a frivolous distraction."

A thread of lightness entered Emmeline's voice. "Then

I command you to do it. Ser Kahldar often takes the grave-yard shift for himself."

With immense effort, Selida dipped another curtsey. "Very well. I shall do my best to ensure that Ser Kahldar does not perish of either cold or boredom upon the battlements."

"Let it give you something hopeful to think about."

Selida closed her lips. *A serpent would sooner share a rabbit with a wolf.* But she held her pose until the door closed with a soft click and she was, again, alone.

CHAPTER
FIVE

Selida extended her palms as the young couple stepped over the bowl of beaten silver. The youth, a fisherman by his calluses, and the girl, round with child, blushed so hard at each other that they did not notice. Deftly, Selida caught their free hands in hers.

"The serpents of the sky bind you." Selida sang the words twice, translating the ancient Elven ceremony for its present-day participants. "For as long as you love and protect each other, Aluna will bless you with the abundance of the sea."

"Blessings return to you tenfold, Lady Cleric," the girl said. She released Selida's hand to fumble in her pockets. "Our offering—"

"Aluna will take your offerings in prayers this season, sister."

As the happy couple returned to their family, Selida peered down the thronged hallway. Tidelanders—standing, sitting, and holding shells—extended all the way to the staircase.

Selida pursed her lips. At first, she had wondered what subtle strategy Emmeline might employ to keep her seditious cleric in check. Now it was obvious. *Idle hands are the devils' workshop,* she imagined the lady murmuring to herself. And so, while Selida hauled her saddlebags from the stable up to the chapel, Emmeline had rushed Dame Pottage into starting dinner half an hour early. Every single refugee had therefore been present to watch as Selida took her place at Lydris's right.

By the time Selida had entertained Lydris through his dessert of dried fruit, dozens of Tidelanders had found their way to the new chapel's door, eager for sacraments interrupted by their unseasonal relocation to Wyvernsvow.

Many faces were familiar to her, so it was with a sense of inevitability that Selida opened the door after dinner and heard five confessions, dispensed penance—why, yes, Aluna demands that you apologize to your brother— and performed name day rituals for two babies. Then this wedding. *Tidemother keep you all.*

Before she could admit a mother and her young daughter into the chapel, she heard a sharp voice crackle down the hallway from the stairs. "Off with you all, now. Lady Selida still has work to do this evening. There'll be time enough tomorrow to confess your woes."

It was Lydris's nurse, Old Meg. Her gray head appeared at the end of the passage as she began shuffling people back down the way they'd come. In her left hand she carried a lantern.

Selida waited until the hallway was clear. "What work, now?"

Old Meg grinned and held out a sachet of tea. "My lady's orders to walk the wall, of course. You can find the kettle downstairs, in the kitchen."

"She wants me to start tonight?"

"Aye." The nurse lifted the lantern, and fiddled with its door. "Methinks you'll need this as well. Won't do to keep our kin waiting in the dark."

Selida stilled. Meg had been Emmeline's nurse too, decades ago, and remained fiercely proud of her long service to the Skyfawn family. When Selida and Laurence had trailed Lord Coralglass to the Tidelander royal palace, Meg had braided shells into their hair and kept watch as they ottered around in the surf. Now, Selida picked her words carefully. "Do you mean for me to pass them some message?"

"Ach, lass, these bones are too old to know what the lads want to hear these days." She patted Selida on the cheek, fingers like withered roses. "I'm only here to help you do what your faith tells you must be done."

Selida stiffened. "I'm afraid, Mistress, that Aluna teaches us wisdom by holding Her own counsel."

Meg shook her head and left the lantern on the floor by the door. "Do as you like, so long as you do *something*. Is that not what your father used to say?" She gave a sour smile. "The old shark never stopped swimming, I'll give him that much."

Selida glowered at the lantern as the nurse disappeared down the hallway. Then she looked down at her fingers, clenched around the tea pouch. *There is more than one way to end a siege.* She returned to her trunk for a warm cloak. *Perhaps Ser Kahldar will prove more reasonable surrounded by the cold stones of his keep.*

The stairs to the parapet narrowed as they rose. The fog had receded, exposing an endless dome of stars. As Selida stepped into the knife-sharp cold, the black ocean spread around her, reflecting the Tidelands' thousand constellations like a glittering cape. Landwards, a few campfires burned in the scrub at the top of the rise. She kept the open door of Meg's lantern pointed away from them as she carried the kettle along the parapet to the first of the guardsmen on the wall.

He was, of course, the squire with the broken nose.

"Tea?" Selida lowered the lantern and proffered the mug she had brought with her.

He looked at her and took a quick step backwards. His hands rose, palms out.

"Very well. Perhaps tomorrow."

The next guardsman huddled under a torch twenty feet away. Beyond him stood another. From here, she could see so many men on the wall that the whole of it seemed bathed in light.

It was going to be a long night.

From his post, Kahldar watched a distant figure emerge onto the wall. His brow furrowed; the changing of the guard had just occurred, with all men properly accounted for. Had Ser Aegison sent a messenger with news? But no, they did not carry one of the keep's standard lanterns.

After a few moments' scrutiny, he realized with a start that he knew exactly who the newcomer was. Even at this distance, it was impossible to mistake her fluid gait—or the manner in which Squire Penson recoiled from her. A grimly satisfied smile crossed Kahldar's face; the boy, it seemed, had learned his lesson.

Still, watching Selida make her way along the parapet, Kahldar reminded himself that he had erred almost as calamitously during his first year at Wyvernsvow. True, his mistake was one of invitation rather than imposition —*Was Penson raised in a cave?*—but it too was born of unfamiliarity with the ways of the Tidelands.

It had just been so exhilarating, he remembered, to emerge triumphant in the tourney last fall. This, he had thought, must be what those heroes out of song once felt. How right and proper, then, to offer the crown upon his lance to the recently-arrived lady cleric whose timeless beauty brought to mind myths and legends.

Selida, of course, did not hail from his people's epics but

from the Tidelands. What he had intended as a chivalrous display of esteem, she had taken as an expression of carnal interest. And when she had sought him out in the stables... the memory still made Kahldar shiver. Never before or since had he come so dangerously close to forsaking his vows.

Every encounter with her thereafter had been fraught with embarrassment and confusion, until finally he had retreated behind a barricade of frosty, formal civility. This had done nothing to dissuade her attentions, but it at least afforded him some measure of solid footing, and a reminder of what was expected of him—what he expected of himself.

Some part of Kahldar had hoped this autumn might afford him an opportunity to correct the mistakes of the year previous, to explain what had been in his heart on the day of the joust. But now, with the keep besieged, it would be a foolish vanity to indulge such selfish whims. And so, as the stars wheeled above, he renewed his fortifications and braced to receive the woman slowly but inexorably approaching his position.

The Coiled Viper was arcing directly overhead by the time Selida located Kahldar. Standing at the prow of Wyvernsvow's easternmost tower, wearing only a light cloak over his plate, he frowned silently out at the embers on the rise.

"You walked a thorough path along the parapet."

Below them, on a lower wall, men were ceding their places to the next shift.

His profile cheered her beyond good reason. "Why, Ser Kahldar, were you waiting for me?"

"I prefer my tea hot."

Selida poured the last of the fragrant water from the kettle and offered him the mug. His open posture made her think he found the air balmy, compared to the killing ice of the Dawnlands. She wondered what he would say if she asked him to thaw her numb fingers by rolling them in his palms. His mouth flattened as if he could read her thoughts on her face. Instead of taking the mug from her, he pointed to a flat spot on the wall between them.

Rolling her eyes, she obliged. Then she pulled her arms under her cloak and crossed them over her breasts. "Will your Welded chastity unravel if we brush fingertips? Should I be flattered?"

"Have I not asked you to cease your distractions?" He nodded out at the darkness. "Those campfires belong to the Fox. His men grow in number every day. They will make their intentions clear very soon. Perhaps today."

"Excellent." Selida slid him a glance. "Then we can parlay. Maybe the farmers will get back to their fields in time to salvage what's left of the harvest."

She felt his eyes brush her features, like a blind man reading her expression. "Is that what you asked of Lady Magnus?"

"We spoke of other things."

"Ah." Finally, he took a sip of tea. "She rejected your petition."

Selida resisted the urge to grind her teeth. "An unfortunate setback." She forced some humility into her voice; forced her eyes to meet his. "So I came to ask you a question. Under what terms do you think Wyvernsvow might reach parlay with the Fox?"

His lips parted in surprise. Kahldar's expression softened, and he answered with a mixture of sympathy and regret: "None."

She blinked. "Nonsense. All we require are two people who can agree to not kill each other."

He stared into his mug. "By His Majesty's long-standing decree, ancient treasures—especially those of a magical nature—belong to the Dominion entire. The royal bailiff sees to it that they are distributed fairly, based on need. And the Dominion does not negotiate with bandits."

Heat prickled in her chest and she took a step closer to him. "The *Dominion* may not deign to treat with bandits, but if this castle eats the entire harvest before winter begins, everyone in the keep will be dead by spring. Surely avoiding that fate justifies some creative parsing of your King's mandates."

She saw him consider and discard many words. "You would do better to focus your energy on matters within your gift, Lady Cleric. Many of our refugees are anxious for reassurance. Perhaps tomorrow you might extend special prayers for the young men conscripted this summer."

Selida felt her lips tighten even as she struggled to pitch her voice low. She pointed to a youth, down still soft on his face, standing at attention by the postern gate. "Do not expect Aluna to endorse your madness. That child would have better spent his summer fishing or farming."

"If the Fox had not fomented insurrection upon hearing of the treasure, the boy would have been free to do exactly that."

Her other hand found his bracer. It was ice under her fingertips, but the wrist beneath jumped at her touch before steadying into unyielding granite. "If your people were not about to carry it away, disgruntled Tidelanders would not feel it worth their lives to reclaim it." She stared up at him, half glower, half plea. "Consider what a treasure, found in the ruins of one of our temples, might mean to us."

"Us?"

Her face started to burn. "Yes, *us*. Our ancestors practiced great magic. Artifacts in that trove may show us visions of what has been. Others may deepen our connection to Aluna Herself." Selida turned her face away from him to stare at the sea. "When Ser Aegison announced he was turning the lot, unseen and uncatalogued, over to the Dominion, years of resignation solidified into panic. And what will King Harald do with it, anyway? Melt it all into yet more of those endless coins that bear his face?"

"Common coinage facilitates trade."

She glared at him. "Do you *hear* yourself?"

He let her breathe. Then, his free gloved hand came over hers. Gently: "Must you still harbor resentment? When I was a child, the people of my mountain pass could only dream of having as much to eat as your coastal communities do today."

Bile rose in her throat. "When *I* was a child, our fishermen slept under blankets of cerulean wool and wore pearls to market. Now I must beg our young people to forswear banditry, or else end their days strung up for the crows. Resentment does not *begin* to describe what I feel."

"Ah." He stared another moment at where her hand touched his bracer, and then gingerly moved it aside. His tone stiffened, approaching scholarly abstraction. "According to the howls of your neighbors, past generations of Tidelanders won most of their wealth through piracy. Now the Dominion demands that you put an end to pillaging and instead take up lawful trade." He looked out over the peninsula. "Wealth could return to the Tidelands, if you were to apply yourselves."

Selida resisted the urge to grab his shoulders and shake. *Why, why, why* had she thought this a reasonable gambit? Every time they fell into any true conversation, one which touched on anything that actually mattered, she was reminded: It was far more enjoyable to tease him until his beautiful features flushed. If she could not have his passion, his ire would have to do.

Fire that only blood can quench. She tried one more time. "Very well. You dismiss our concerns and consider our ways criminal. Even so, surely you see that the treasure gives you the upper hand in any parlay with the Fox. Why not attempt to reason with him?"

His gaze remained on the horizon. "It is hard for me to imagine a dialogue that would not feed the brewing rebellion."

She took three deep breaths. "Fine. What if we offered *lawfully obtained* Dominion currency in exchange for the historical artifacts found under the keep? Your King would retain the magical items for his distribution, as well as the overall value of Lord Lydris's discovery."

"Assuming the keep's treasury could afford to do so, would your people be satisfied with that?"

"The Church would encourage the Tidelands to see the treasure as a sign that the future grows atop the legacy of the past, instead of requiring its annihilation."

He tilted his head. "And this would keep Aluna central to your people, deflecting the influence of the Welded Church?"

She lifted her chin.

Kahldar pondered this for several long seconds. "Having sworn to do my utmost to see this keep safely through the siege, I find some merit in your proposal."

Her lips parted. "You astonish me. I thought you said it was impossible."

He returned his gaze to her. "It may yet be. You would first have to persuade the King's representatives that releasing Tidelander treasures would not reignite civil war."

"*Tidemother*—was I not clear this afternoon, on the road? My people are forbidden to make war on their relatives, on pain of excommunication."

"Clearly, that does nothing to prevent conflict with sufficiently distant cousins. Had your noble families managed to resist fighting among themselves long enough to uphold their initial treaty with the Dominion half a century ago, His Majesty would not have needed to pacify the coast."

She wondered what would happen if she punched his breastplate. Her hand would hurt, probably, and he would feel nothing. "Oh, so you did it for the *people*, and not for a rich port and its taxes?"

"We very much needed access to the port, and King Carlon bargained for that through diplomacy. Conquest was only deemed necessary after the third time a new Tidelander family seized control of the city and refused to honor the terms agreed to by those they had displaced. When King Harald finally put an end to the chaos which had long plagued this land, taxes were necessary to provide security for its people. Half your villages didn't even have roads."

She could not help herself. "The *ocean* is our road. The Serpent of the Sea calms at Aluna's command."

He shrugged. "Once the paved thoroughfares are finished, you won't need to rely on your goddess in order to travel safely. In a generation, I expect your mothers will feel relieved that their children no longer need brave the dangers of open water."

Her voice dropped, venomously sweet. "Why, Ser Kahldar, have you still not learned to swim?"

A clank of approaching footsteps made them both straighten. Kahldar took a step away from her. Selida opened her clenched hands and dried them against her side.

Ser Aegison frowned at them both. "Lady Cleric. You were given permission to bring tea to the men, not distribute blandishments."

"I often accomplish two things at once. Is that difficult for you?"

Kahldar dropped the wooden mug and took half a step between Selida and his commander.

Ser Aegison purpled. He opened his mouth to bellow, but at that moment they all saw it: a flurry of movement on the ridge just as the eastern sky began to lighten. A small cavalcade of riders thundered down the road towards the keep.

Selida strained her eyes, but she'd spent all of Aluna's gifts earlier in the evening. Now, she could see only black-painted shields, and lance banners bereft of crests and colors. Dispossessed Tidelander knights, she judged, riding with the fluid ease of her people.

Ser Aegison's shout stopped a disorganized stampede along the walls. Conscripted archers scrambled for quivers.

The knot of riders halted well out of shortbow range. Three put curved horns to their lips. Then—a long trill of notes. The liquid chorus began as an effortless warble of *golondrinas*, and ended as a pugnacious bugle of defiance.

The sound closed around her heart like a mailed fist. Her eyes closed too, and she was suddenly a little girl again, standing beside her father, listening to the last glories of their doomed realm.

"What does it mean?" Ser Aegison huffed. "What are they saying?"

Kahldar answered: "It is a declaration of war." When Selida opened her eyes in surprise—*How had he known?*—she realized he was watching her face, and had read the truth in her expression.

Then Kahldar was ducking back from the parapet; in an instinctive gesture, he shoved her behind himself and away from the wall. "They're firing arrows."

Ser Aegison turned on his heel and began to bark orders.

"Lady Cleric," Kahldar said, pushing Selida firmly towards the stairs, "please go inside. It has begun."

CHAPTER
SIX

"The guardsmen say they saw a shower of arrows, but none overtopped the walls." The village headwoman from yesterday, lately drafted into Dame Pottage's service, dropped a stack of dirty bowls on the counter. "The morning guard rotation is coming in now."

"To think it would come to this." Dame Pottage wrung her apron. "Lady Cleric, is that double batch of scones ready?"

"Yes ma'am," Selida said as she folded dried currants into a bowl of batter. A light touch was all they wanted— no more than three turns of the spatula or the scones would bake leaden. She murmured a prayer and the coil of dough inflated, as Goddess-sent milk and flour bolstered the other ingredients.

"They say they'll use that big crossbow as soon as they have summat to aim it at."

Selida removed a pan of scones from the oven. Her fingers trembled. The long night had left her too jagged to sleep. Ser Kahldar had remained on the wall; she should use this time to hammer her thoughts on parlay into a spear she might wedge sideways into Ser Aegison's prejudices.

What must I say, to make them listen?

The two little girls appeared behind their mother's skirts. As Selida handed them fresh scones, she heard Ser Aegison's footsteps thunder into the great hall. He called for young Lord Lydris.

Now.

She still did not know what to say. It did not matter; if she waited until blood had been spilt, parlay would recede beyond reach. Selida forced herself to pause at the edge of the kitchen. Her limbs shook as if she swam with Aluna's coldfire eels. *Ugh.* She took a moment to smooth her hair, remove her apron, and pick up the basket of scones she'd set aside earlier. Then she took a deep breath and slid into the great hall.

"—claims that the Fox wants nothing to do with the castle, so long as we turn over the treasure." Ser Aegison gesticulated with a strip of paper that curled as if recently unwound from the leg of a bird. Kahldar stood behind him, face composed into tree-trunk neutrality. Selida's teeth set.

Lydris, flushed with excitement, sat in the lord's chair, his mother beside him. "So he'll just turn around and go away if we give it to him?"

"I would not trust the word of a man who calls himself 'the Fox.'" Ser Aegison smoothed his moustache. "It is likely a trap. If we lean out a window, they'll be upon us like crows after a bit of glass."

Selida approached the high table. She used a pair of tongs to offer Lydris a scone she'd topped with precious shavings of orange peel. "I have a question, my lord, if you would hear it." She glanced at Emmeline, who was stirring her son's porridge.

Emmeline considered, and then nodded. Lydris, watching her, followed suit.

Selida ducked her head. "Thank you. Ser Kahldar has explained to me that the Dominion uses a common currency, so that all coins are interchangeable."

"Is there a question here?" Ser Aegison interrupted.

"Given the state of the harvest and the inexperience of your conscripts, would you consider parlay? You could offer the Fox and his followers a piece or three of treasure; whichever you judge to have the greatest historical value. In exchange, you would ask him to depart peacefully. I am sure he does not wish for the people of the coast to starve either."

Ser Aegison gave her a look that could have flayed leather. "You would cheat the King of his due?"

Selida bent over the table to serve Emmeline her scone. "You could give His Majesty coins from Wyvernsvow's treasury in place of what you offered the besiegers." She dared not glance at Ser Kahldar, but she silently urged him to add his voice to the debate.

Ser Aegison did not give him an opportunity. "Your understanding of His Majesty's laws is lamentably narrow." He turned to Lady Magnus. "My lady. Control your creature."

"Lady Cleric," Emmeline said, deadpan, "thank you for breakfast. You are dismissed."

Selida could not help herself; she glowered at Ser Kahldar. His expression remained tree-stump dead. She tightened her hands on the basket to suppress the urge to transform all the wooden spoons in the hall into adders. Then she turned to Lydris, curtseying to give herself a moment to smooth down the raw edge in her voice. "As your mother wishes, my lord. But I beg you: Consider what might best keep your people safe."

Ser Aegison snapped a short bow. "Your lady mother may be your regent, my lord, but King Harald himself put the safety of your keep in my hands. I promise you I will see all its people through this siege."

Lydris turned intent eyes on Selida. "Ser Aegison said earlier that the arrows can only reach halfway up the wall. That means nobody in the keep should come to harm, even if we do not engage in parlay."

"They may yet find a better angle and outlook for their archers," Kahldar said. *Finally.* "And they are not likely to tire. Based on their campfires, their numbers swell daily."

"Cheap tricks, belike," Ser Aegison said.

Selida ignored him. "My lord, your conscripted men have little experience yet. If we allow the siege to progress to bloodshed, they will suffer the worst of the injuries, and flagging morale may tempt them to foolishness. A prompt end to this siege, on the other hand, guarantees strong hands for next spring's planting and fishing. Countless mothers, sisters, and wives would bless your name."

Parlay, she willed silently. *Parlay, parlay, parlay.*

Emmeline held up a hand: "Ser Aegison, is it not true that the King's men will be on the road before the month ends?"

"Absolutely true, milady."

"And even if our stores run low, do you think the men on the road are a danger to our fishing boats?"

"Absolutely not, milady."

Lady Magnus sat back in her chair and glanced pointedly at Selida.

Selida softened her lips. "Fall storms may yet hamper both their reinforcements and our fishermen."

"Your storms are nothing compared to the Dawnlands' blizzards," Ser Aegison scoffed.

"Then I believe we are done here," Emmeline said. She took up her spoon.

Flushing, Selida curtseyed to the table before turning back towards the kitchens. As she passed Ser Kahldar, she shoved the basket of scones into his hands.

She savored his one, surprised inhalation before the great hall disappeared from view. Citrus, she remembered, was one of his favorite scents.

Ser Aegison's voice rose over the heartbeats thundering against her eardrums. "Rest assured, my lord: They are treasure mad. We must not trust anything they say."

"Well, sounds like you did your best, Lady Cleric." Dame Pottage placed a basket beside Selida's workstation. "Put the choppings here when you're done?"

Selida lined the onions up under her cleaver and blinked away the smarting. Her tongue trembled with all the things she now wished she had said differently.

"Ser Aegison's a frustrating one, he is," the older woman commiserated. Then: "If you chop any harder, you're like to split the cutting board along with the onions."

Before Selida could promise to mend it later, she heard the rest of the kitchen fall into silence. When she looked up, young Lydris was standing in the doorway leading to the hall.

"Please continue," he said, his high voice cutting through the fragrant air. Then, followed by his mother, he bounced down to Selida's station at the long table.

Selida put down the knife, wiped onion tears on the stole at her shoulder, and bowed her head.

"My lord?"

His brown eyes searched her blotchy red face. "Are you still upset, Lady Cleric?"

Selida glanced at Emmeline. The woman's expression was transparent: *See how wise my son has grown?*

Selida wanted to shake her.

"Yes, my lord," she managed instead. This crisis would tax the wisdom of someone five times this child's age and experience. Her heart wished Lydris were free of the keep, the siege, and all his blighted inheritance... but he was here, and events might yet depend on whatever discernment he could muster. "I am worried that if we do nothing but wait for rescue, terrible hunger will be the least of our people's problems."

"The royal taxmen will be here before that happens," he said. "But, because you are upset, I will write a letter asking for more aid, and send it by pigeon today."

"Ser Aegison says a show of force might persuade the bandits to scatter," Emmeline murmured.

So he and his ilk can round up the survivors and string them up in all our town squares? The Dawnlanders outdid even her own people's appetite for escalation.

Selida curtseyed. "Thank you for your consideration, my lord. If you do write, I beg you stress haste. If reinforcements arrive before fighting starts in earnest, the Fox may stand down. He seeks your treasure, not a bloodbath."

"I shall use your words directly."

She swallowed. "It does my heart proud to see you grow into your responsibilities."

He straightened. "I have something else for you. Perhaps this will cheer your thoughts." As she watched, his smile broadened to fit his child's face. "Give me your hands."

Selida wiped them on a towel. The boy reached into

his velvet surcoat and dropped a single gold coin into her cupped palms. It was heavy and oblong, nearly the size of her thumb. A woman's profile graced one side, with long pointed ears and curling hair. The metal edges undulated in the ancient Elven style, delicate work once common in coin from across the sea. She imagined it melting, Aluna's likeness blurring into King Harald's.

Tidemother. Do not make me long to hurt them.

Lydris bounced on his toes. "We no longer allow anyone to see the treasure, but Ser Aegison let me keep this piece. There are many others like it below. You may study it, while you remain here."

Selida glanced at Emmeline, who nodded. She turned back to Lord Lydris and curtseyed. "You are too kind." Gently, she turned the coin over. She could still smell the salt of the tidepools on it. On this side, tiny ships chased waves and dolphins.

"Perhaps if you pray to Aluna, She can tell you stories about it?"

"I will let you know if She does."

Lydris's voice dropped into childish longing. "Can you show me the snakes now?"

Behind her son, Emmeline shook her head.

Selida paused. "Now that the siege has started, I'm afraid I may need Aluna's servants to heal your men should the fighting become dangerous."

"Oh." Lydris's golden head drooped. Then he perked up. "May I have another blandishment instead, then?"

Selida blinked. "Pardon?"

"That is what Ser Kahldar said you distribute." He sent a pointed glance at a tray of scones cooling over the stove. "Maybe one that is plain? I don't like dried fruit."

Selida swallowed a smile. "Certainly."

Emmeline looked amused. "Is that what we're calling them now?"

He would hate it.

She adopted a tone of casual innocence. "Evidently."

SEVEN

Selida walked the parapet, tray in one hand and lantern in the other, its open door pointed squarely towards the inner baily. Aluna's coin bumped against her thigh, ocean-cool even through the pocket of her split skirts. Her divinations had revealed its age—ancient—along with an impression of its maker and glimpses of its recent associates: her own vestments, Lydris's wooden toys, and glittering heaps of goblets and jewelry. Atop one such pile rested a rune-inscribed pearl.

What is Your will now, *Tidemother?*

Three days had passed since the Fox sent his missive. Each night, ever more guards stood on the walls, walked the halls, and watched over the larders. To assuage their growing anxiety, more and more of the faithful crowded outside her chapel door. This morning, the line had stretched down the stairs. Selida halted on an empty span where the wall turned away from the land and towards the half of the keep that jutted out over the ocean. She closed her eyes, and savored the silence.

Unfamiliar ships had appeared on the horizon earlier that day, scuttling the keep's plan to send fishermen out in boats to restock the larder. Now Selida saw only darkness. The air bit her cheeks and nose; she had left her wrap inside, hoping that the cold would preempt yet another night of sleeplessness.

Where were the campfires?

Selida had just a moment to consider the thought before defenders on the landward wall shouted alarm. Dropping the lantern, she dumped the iron kettle off the tray and ran towards the sound.

By the time Selida could see the chaos, most of the men had retreated under the shelter of one of the guard towers. Holding the tray like a shield, she sprinted the last thirty feet across the stonework. An arrow sang through the air inches from her shoulder.

A panicked guardsman turned to her. "He's shot through the neck—of all the wave-cursed ill fortune—"

Selida shoved him aside. "Let me see."

A young man lay on the floor. He held an arrow pressed to his throat. His lips burbled red. *Not Kahldar.* Selida sank to the planks beside him. "Serpent of the Sea attend me," she called, as she wrapped one hand around the arrow shaft. The other she placed over his slick skin so that the half-submerged arrowhead pricked between her first and second fingers. She could feel the snakes coiled in his blood thrashing in panic.

As if her thoughts had summoned him, Kahldar appeared in the guardhouse. "A party with ladders approaches the south wall. They likely—" Upon seeing Selida with the wounded man on the floor, he knelt abruptly at her side.

"Hold his head still," she ordered. His hands, strong and steady, closed over her patient's temples. Selida drew a deep breath, and released the flood of prayer as she jerked the arrowhead free.

Blood—black in the torchlight—fountained everywhere: over her hands, over his face, over her blue robes. Aluna's magic, too, suffused them all, and the surface of the young man's mangled throat writhed, smoothed, and grew still. And then he took a deep, gasping breath.

Selida exhaled in relief. "Who else?"

Kahldar stood with a bow of gratitude. "No more here." He directed his attention outwards. "Men, ready your swords, shields, and spears. We go to the south wall. Lady Selida, if you would return to the central bailey. There may be other wounded."

He was gone again, the rest of the soldiers clanking behind him.

The young man at her knee gave a grunt and made to push himself up to follow. Selida placed a hand on his chest. "You nearly perished," she said. "Rest a moment before you split your knit flesh."

He looked up at her in mingled awe and horror.

"You'll live, if you're careful." She rose. "Use a shield next time."

The night sortie ended minutes later. Among the keep's guardsmen and their three captured assailants, Selida catalogued one concussion, one crushed hand, and several worrying lacerations. Kahldar bid her heal the worst two where they lay. The rest, his men carried to the chapel where she now boiled water and prepared salve, needles, and thread.

"But you're injured," she said to Kahldar. Blood darkened his leathers from an arrow that had pierced the mail just under his pauldron.

He winced, as if only now noticing how he favored his left arm. "It is nothing."

They had not spoken since breakfast, three days ago, but she had felt him watching her whenever their paths intersected. Most of the time, he turned away before she could catch him at it. Now, her hand reached out as if she could feel the shape of the injury under the fabric. "Then be gentle until I can call upon more of Aluna's blessings tomorrow."

He let her hand rest on his arm for only a moment before taking a breath, and then stepping back. "I... appreciate your concern. Nonetheless, these men may be of aid to us. See to them first."

Selida tied off a thread. The oozing hole in her patient's side would not likely lead to gangrene, but she would check again tomorrow to be sure.

Old Meg stood beside her, hands full of bandages. "You lost the lantern, I see."

Selida exhaled silently. "It was a waste of time."

The nurse sighed. "That was all I had, and there will be no more post, not with the roads closed. What do you mean to do next?"

Selida put the needle down and met the old woman's pale eyes. "Aluna guides me, Mistress. Rest your tired bones, and worry no more about it."

Relief flickered across the weathered face. "You're a good girl, Selida."

"Father would not agree."

Old Meg snorted. "Begging your pardon, Lady, but he was an arse."

Ser Aegison's strident footsteps filled the hall outside. Selida swallowed her curse and reached for the linens as Lydris's nurse faded out the open door.

"Kahldar, are the prisoners in hand?"

"Aye, Ser." He bowed his superior into the chapel.

"By Exos, man, we hardly need *her* to minister to this scum. Their place is in the gaol."

"As you command, Ser. But their wounds should not go untreated."

"Clean up their injuries, if you wish, but I'll not have you wasting your scant prayers upon them." Selida looked up to find Ser Aegison glowering at her. "They chose to attack, and they can very well live—or not—with the consequences of their actions."

Alarm blared through Selida's chest. "Holding a man without healing him is a form of torture."

"Oh, we shall get to that too, in good time."

The patient whimpered.

Selida straightened. "Aluna does not approve. Hold them whole, if you wish, for leverage with the Fox, or let them go."

"No wonder your people have never managed to keep peace in these lands."

"And you have?"

"We shall, by Exoeras." Ser Aegison turned his glower on Kahldar. "See these men taken below. Drag them there yourself if you must." He turned on his heel.

Kahldar stepped between Selida and his commander before she could surge to her feet. "Lady Cleric," he said, and gestured to the prisoners. "Once you are finished, I will accompany these men to the cellars."

Selida bit her lip, hard, and ducked her head so his expression would not make her want to claw at him. "I suppose you must do as you see fit."

His voice seemed somehow distant. "As must we all."

Kahldar stood at the parapet where he had captured the Fox's agents the night before. Morning mist rose off the water, turning the fresh light of Exos a soft golden rose.

"Excellent work." Ser Aegison paced up the wall beside him, staring out at the peninsula. Campfire smoke smudged the horizon. "Your watch flanked the miscreants before they could breach the bailey, despite their archers' distraction."

Kahldar frowned. "Even so, it troubles me that the Fox's men were able to surmount this stretch of wall. I would have expected the loose boulders below to foil their ladders." His eyes lingered on the shattered remains of Selida's lantern. He had kicked it, along with her kettle, into a gutter during the fight. "I also wonder why they led with saps, instead of steel. Only after we cornered them did they fight in earnest."

"Poverty? Overconfidence?" Ser Aegison shrugged dismissively. "We'll extract it from them, one way or another."

Kahldar turned his head towards the ocean, and held his silence.

Ser Aegison spat over the edge. "I will not limit myself to half measures while the castle's safety is at stake."

Kahldar let the seconds pass. He counted five.

Ser Aegison sighed. "Very well. You need not concern yourself with the interrogations. You were up most of the night, and injured. Take the morning. Go downstairs. Have a hot breakfast. Finch should re-check your shoulder."

Kahldar acknowledged this with a nod. He let his commander's footsteps recede off the parapet. Only when the man had gone did he reach down and pull Selida's kettle out of the gutter.

In truth, Kahldar had slept little, even after the

sergeant had cleaned and bound his wound. Instead, he lay remembering Selida's stony glower as she saw him out of her chapel. His mind worried over what it meant, and what it might yet portend. He dreamed of it, and of more... of what might have happened had he stayed, and allowed her to treat his injury.

Balance in thought, word, and deed. But even when he fixed the teachings of Exoeras in his mind, they could not quiet his body. Her presence made him ache with a turmoil he thought he had outgrown, as though she were the answer to a question he dared not even think.

Perhaps he would find her at breakfast, he thought, starting towards the great hall. It would be reassuring to see her sitting beside Lady Magnus, entertaining the young lord with stories.

She was not yet there. The cavernous room was warm from the fire, and fragrant with eggs and porridge. Kahldar stepped into a stream of guardsmen and let himself vanish into the blizzard of their boisterous conversation.

"—another attack?"

Kahldar blinked. One of the younger knights had spoken to him. He replayed the last few moments of dialogue in his mind. *Ah.*

"If we increase our numbers on the wall this morning, we will not be rested should they launch an attack later in the day. Tell your men to keep to the schedule we've practiced, and let the Fox do the work of coming to us."

When he arrived at his usual seat, Kahldar found his eye drawn to the scone that sat on his plate.

"What is this?"

"Oh, do you not want it?" A young guardsman, one of the summer's conscripted recruits, straightened hopefully. "It is one of Lady Selida's blandishments. She left just enough for all of us."

Kahldar felt his back teeth set. "What did you say?"

"That's what she called them. I'm not sure how she manages to bake them so tall, but they're wonderfully fluffy." He pursed his lips wistfully.

"Aluna blesses us through Her clerics," an older Tidelander guardsman said. "As in the story of the loaves and eels, She extends our stores even as She fills the cisterns and heals our wounds."

The first young man was still staring at the scone on Kahldar's plate. "It's a divine blandishment?"

Kahldar scanned the hall again. Selida's place at the high table, by Lord Lydris and Lady Magnus, still sat empty. Alarm bells sounded in the back of his mind and his chest was suddenly heavy with dread. "Excuse me," he said.

"Do you not want yours?" the younger man called after him.

"Her blandishments?" He strode for the cellar caves they had converted, last night, into an impromptu gaol. "No. You are welcome to them."

EIGHT

As Kahldar jogged down the irregular tunnels, Selida's voice ricocheted up to him: "Ransom these men back to the Fox if you must, but stay your barbaric Dawnland tortures. I have just healed them, and by the Law of Salvage, their flesh belongs to the Goddess. Aluna will not have it."

Ser Aegison, furious: "Did I not command you last night not to waste your prayers on them?"

"I obey Aluna's will in these matters, not yours."

"Then it is fortunate for Wyvernsvow that, within the Dominion, matters of security exceed the purview of the Church. For the last time, Cleric: stand aside."

Kahldar stepped into the makeshift gaol to find Selida blocking the doorway of a stone cell, arms spread. Today she wore her teal vestments and tide-colored stole, but not her breastplate. Her hair, done up in its customary loops, glowed in the torchlight, and deep purple shadows sat under her eyes. He could feel invisible serpents seething in the air around her. Behind her, last night's prisoners stirred, still bound. Before her stood Ser Aegison and three other guardsmen. The knight commander's blade remained in its sheath, but his hand hovered ominously near it. The others, Dawnlanders all, exchanged glances.

Kahldar pitched his voice to a quiet carry. "Lady Selida," he said, "these men attacked us last night."

She did not turn her head, but he saw her eyes dart to him before returning to focus on Ser Aegison. "They did not kill any of you."

Ser Aegison's lips curled back on his teeth. "Not for lack of trying."

"You have not killed any of them, either," Selida said. "Without casualties, last night's sortie is a mere misunderstanding between neighbors." She lowered her voice to a cool, soothing tide. "Just—arrange to speak with the Fox. Then all of this will fade into memory."

Ser Aegison tensed in a way Kahldar knew presaged violence. "There will be no conversation with bandits," he declared. "And I will not risk the safety of this castle for your foolish Tideland traditions. *Someone* told these men where and how to strike last night. They, and the secrets they possess, belong to the King."

The lithe muscles in Selida's pale arms sprang out against her skin as she braced herself in the doorway. Her chin dropped. "Then have your King come down to collect them himself," she hissed. "Or does he only wield the lash through his dogs?"

"*Selida,*" Kahldar snapped, before Ser Aegison could draw. As he strode forward, he willed her hypnotic gaze to meet his. "Selida, think. If another attack catches us unawares, innocent lives may be lost. It is our duty to safeguard those who have come to us for protection. To do that, we must know what these men know."

She stood her ground as he closed the distance between them. "Then ask them *civilly.*"

"If we do, will they answer truthfully?" he inquired. He was standing a handsbreadth from her now, Ser Aegison behind him.

Her aqua eyes blazed. "Would *you*, if you were in their position?"

"Perhaps, if my Gods so compelled me."

He saw her lips twitch, but she bowed her head a fraction. "Such rituals require preparation." A moment of silence, then: "I could ready one for you tomorrow."

He frowned, keeping his voice gentle. "Time is a luxury we do not have. Who else will you risk by having us delay?"

"Send a reply to the Fox," she said. *Was that a thread of supplication in her voice?* "He will not press his attack if you show some willingness to negotiate."

"Enough." Ser Aegison stepped forward. "Ser Kahldar, remove Lady Selida from my presence."

She stared up at him.

"My apologies," Kahldar said.

He saw her jaw tighten, witnessed the exact moment when her emotions overwhelmed her good sense. *Oh.* Her rising anger had been obvious, but the flicker of desperation in her eyes surprised him; was this the same woman who met every rebuke and offense with casual self-assurance? The revelation made him more sympathetic, not less, as she snapped her fingers and turned the torches to snakes, plunging the room into darkness and chaos.

Standing at parade rest just inside the closed doorway, Kahldar watched Selida pace the length of the chapel. Her quick, irritated steps frothed the hem of her split skirts.

"Come and sit," Lady Magnus said from the chair where she worked at her embroidery. "Since one of the prisoners survived, all will be resolved anon."

Selida was not looking at either of them as she circled. Upon regaining control of the situation, Ser Aegison had ordered the interrogation commence immediately. Though they were now too distant to hear any cries from the cellars, Kahldar knew Selida imagined them; the tendons of her hands flexed as she rubbed her arms. An even more troubling question plagued his imagination: What if Ser Aegison deemed it necessary to interrogate *her*?

Selida frowned at Lady Magnus. "Can't you see that torture is wrong? The slow destruction and perversion of the body?"

"I can see that as a cleric, blessed with the power to heal, you find it particularly disturbing." Lady Magnus patted the chair beside herself. "Come. Your mind will ease if you stop churning to and fro."

Selida ignored her. "Where is Lord Lydris now? Surely you would not let him witness this barbarism."

"Of course not. I left him with Old Meg, so I could come and be here with you."

Kahldar saw Selida struggle with some inner turmoil. Finally, she managed, "You cannot shield him from the truth of this forever. His knight commander is peeling a man in his keep, under his authority, layer by layer. They will hear his screams in the kitchens."

"Such things are not for the eyes of either ladies or children."

"I don't see how Lydris's age or your sex can absolve you of this knowledge."

"If you tried, you might discover new powers and possibilities inherent in both."

"I have seen torture," Kahldar said quietly, before Selida could further undermine her standing with the lady of the keep. "Better that a soldier die on the field than suffer such a fate... or, worse, the betrayal of house and honor that often follows."

The gambit worked; she turned her glower on him. "Of course there was nothing *you* could have done to stop this."

"I could have killed those men last night, rather than

taking them prisoner. But they seemed hesitant to engage, and I do not slay my enemies unless I must."

"Will you show future invaders more lethal mercy, now that you know this is to be their fate?"

"Mayhap."

Her mouth flattened. "I suppose if you were knight commander, you would choose to lash them as well?"

He opened a hand, but not in denial. "There are many reasons I do not seek to lead."

At this Lady Magnus lowered her stitching. "Come, Ser Kahldar—there is loyalty, and then there is false modesty. All men desire command."

"Forgive me, my lady, but no. I do not seek authority; I seek purpose. There is a difference."

Selida's eyes narrowed. "But without authority, you are ever at other people's purposes."

"When our aims are shared, we further our common purpose," Kahldar responded. "I swore to guarantee the safety of the late Lord Magnus's family, and all who shelter in their keep. To this day, I am honored to do so alongside any who seek to do the same."

Selida tossed her head, pivoted on her heel, and started another lap around the chapel.

"Keep the viper in her little blue room," Ser Aegison had barked after they'd killed the snakes, replaced the torches, and beat the sole upright prisoner back into his cell. Kahldar had observed most of this from across the room, having caught up Selida and heaved her over his uninjured shoulder the moment he saw her patience snap. Her weight posed no difficulty, but wrestling her kicking and thrashing form back to the staircase through the pitch-black melee was another matter. Still, as she had unleashed no killing prayers on him, he considered his strategy a success. "You understand?" Ser Aegison had thundered, as Kahldar started up the stairs. "Do not let her out."

Kahldar's exertions had managed to reopen the wound from last night, and now his shoulder throbbed. Ignoring it, he asked, "Are there no orders that you follow, however reluctantly, in Aluna's name? No marriages you perform which you think suspect, no blessings you render upon the unworthy?"

"Aluna allows me to keep my own counsel," Selida snapped. "It is why I chose Her, and not the path my father laid out for me."

"Even so, you serve a Grand Cleric. Where there is worldly power, there are ever orders that must be obeyed."

Her hands clenched. "The Grand Cleric has an eye for character. Her wisdom sends me far away for long periods of time, to do as I judge best."

Lady Magnus sighed. "Selida, there is a peace in obeying another's will, especially if it is a will you trust." Her voice turned gently beseeching. "Perhaps this can be one of those instances."

Before Selida could reply, Kahldar heard Ser Aegison's tread in the hallway. It sounded like half a dozen guardsmen followed in his wake. Kahldar forced his voice to ease. "They are here, milady." Then he opened the door.

Ser Aegison, grim and blood-flecked, filled the frame. He nodded firmly at Kahldar, and then fixed his eyes on Selida.

"You," Ser Aegison said. "Cleric. In addition to obstructing the King's justice, you stand accused of treason against this castle and the Dawnland Dominion. Our prisoner has confessed to your complicity in the attack."

With incredible effort, Kahldar held himself still. Face blank.

Selida's lips writhed with scorn. "Of course he did. You tortured him. He would have renounced the very sea to make you stop."

"He claims it was to your lantern that he and his fellows were instructed to gather on the battlement."

Kahldar, watching her face intently, saw her flinch, though the movement was so slight he was sure none else noticed. "I dropped my lantern to run to the aid of your men."

"You dropped it in a space on the wall empty of guards. Only Ser Kahldar's excellent positioning saw the attackers safely repelled."

"My lantern remained on the wall at that position because there were no men to take it back to the guardhouse."

Lady Magnus had put down her embroidery. "You have an accusation, and a denial from a cleric of the Church." She regarded both Selida and Ser Aegison, her veiled voice regretful. "A cleric who has also healed your men, who refills our cistern and bolsters our larders. What do you propose, Ser?"

"I would like her staked to the courtyard and flogged."

Kahldar watched Selida tense until the bones of her throat stood out like the ribs on a starving deer. A tide of acid rose from his stomach into his chest.

Lady Magnus tilted her head in reproachful bemusement. "Truly, Ser Aegison? The gray area between Aluna's laws and the Dominion's is sufficiently broad to allow us to find a way forward together, do you not think?"

Ser Aegison, red-faced, opened his mouth.

Kahldar cleared his throat. His commander glowered at him, but Kahldar saw in the twitch under his eye that Ser Aegison *did* remember: Yes, the refugees *would* have much to say if their knight commander flogged their cleric.

Ser Aegison's lips pruned. "House arrest, then. Cleric, you are henceforth confined to these quarters. We will bolt your door from the outside to guard against escape or further sabotage."

"Turn Aluna's chapel into a prison?" Lady Magnus still sounded puzzled. "But however shall Lady Selida attend to her duties from here?"

"We can bring the wounded to her."

"And… the cistern?"

"We can bring vessels for her to fill."

Emmeline's gaze grew distant, as if calculating weights and volumes.

Ser Aegison ground his teeth. "Many. Vessels."

A new question creased Lady Magnus's brow. "There is a woman in the stables who is about to give birth. I wonder, can we spare the men to carry her pallet up the stairs to the chapel and then back down for the swaddling?"

"For pity's sake," Selida snapped. "Ser Kahldar is as dense and unyielding as any door. If you insist on this foolishness, then let him be my warden, so that my prison may at least travel with me."

"Ridiculous," Ser Aegison barked.

"Surely you cannot worry that his loyalty could be suborned by my wiles."

"I think it's a lovely idea," Lady Magnus said. She smiled first at Ser Aegison and then at Kahldar. "I feel in my heart that Aluna agrees."

Ser Aegison turned his glower at Kahldar. "You'd be willing to play shepherd to this serpent?"

Kahldar hid the relief in his voice under a dutiful monotone. "As my liege commands."

"Fine," Ser Aegison gritted out. "But she is to be watched at all times, and if her trickery brings down the keep, on your head and honor be it."

Kahldar bowed.

Ser Aegison rounded on Selida. "And you, viper, will keep your mouth to yourself. You are to leave this room *only* if accompanied by Ser Kahldar, Lady Magnus, or myself. You will resume your duties in the kitchen and cistern *only* under our supervision. Is that clear?"

Her lips flattened with rage. "If I wished to harm your men and break this siege, I could blight your provisions and sicken your people. I could fill the barracks with adders." Her voice rose. "Do you think I would play some foolish game with a lantern in the dark?"

"Selida," Kahldar said, "your words are not helping."

Her lips smiled in his direction, but her eyes blazed. "Thank goodness for your presence, Ser Knight. I look forward to more good counsel born of your worldly experience in the *many* long hours to come."

Lady Magnus ignored this outburst. "Lydris must be climbing the walls by now. Selida, could you see to the poor woman in the stables? I fear her child is turned around."

Selida continued to glower at him. "What fun for you."

"After that," Lady Magnus said, "perhaps you could mend Ser Kahldar's shoulder? It's bled through his mail."

The flame of Selida's outrage dimmed slightly as she guiltily inspected his pauldron. Her cheeks now reminded him of his home valley's red autumns, unrepentant in their vibrancy. "You move so easily, I forgot." Then she stepped back, still studying him. "I need to get my kit. One moment."

"I will be here," he said. *And swear to let no harm come to you, or of you.*

Her eyes narrowed, as if she read this unspoken coda in his face. But she turned away all the same, and disappeared behind the altar for her implements.

A stinging rain had turned the courtyard to black mud by the time Kahldar and Selida emerged from the stables. Based on the guard rotation, he guessed it was past midnight. He paused before entering the great hall, wiping water out of his eyes as he waited for her to remember to kick the mud off her shoes.

"You haven't eaten all day," he said at last. "May I fetch you something from the kitchen?"

She looked down at her hands. The torchlight confirmed that they were no longer stained crimson, but Kahldar knew she still saw it: the blood, the baby, the drained mother, the hysterical family.

"I'll eat at breakfast."

Her wan expression silenced his objections. He opened his hand, inviting her to precede him up the stairs.

"I did not know it was possible to safely cut a woman

open, when a birth becomes... difficult," he said. He would never forget the sight of her knife, transformed by her prayers into a blazing sickle of moonlight.

"The cutting open is just the beginning," Selida said. "It is putting everything back the way Aluna intended that renders it an operation of last resort."

This new, horrifying thought gave Kahldar pause. *How many times had a cleric knit two mismatched parts together, with none the wiser until days later?* He softened his voice. "My apologies. I did not mean to call the deed trivial."

"My mother passed from the many complications that follow childbirth. It's likely why midwifery has never been one of my gifts. Growing up, I remember mostly men, embroiled in war."

"I imagine that makes you a diligent attendant, at least."

"Diligence is no substitute for expertise accrued over years, as many a bereaved family could tell you." She paused to rub at a rough patch of masonry. "If this woman had been at home in her village, she might have had any number of better midwives."

"She is alive, and so is her child. How is that not a victory?"

Kahldar watched Selida inspect her nails for blood. Then, she resumed her slow march back up to her chapel. When she spoke, her voice was the merest whisper of sound. "What victory is it to be a baby, born in the Tidelands twenty years into this occupation? Will he meet his end from conscription? Banditry? Torture?"

He did not express the thought which hung over them both: that the birth might have been easier had she not expended so many prayers, fruitlessly, in the dungeon that morning. Instead he replied, "You are unduly dire."

"Am I? Clerics of Aluna offer healing and absolution in exchange for belief and, occasionally, coin. But what that belief actually purchases is reassurance."

"Hope."

"Yes. Hope. And when all hope is exhausted, there is little left for me to do but bear witness to bitterness and pain. Sometimes I think the witnessing is all there is, anymore."

He frowned. "Stop. You are tired, and do not sound like yourself."

She halted on the stairs and pressed a hand over her face. "A convenient accusation, for a Dawnlander."

"Convenient or not, I know despair is not your preferred indulgence."

She gave him a black look. "Why, Ser Kahldar, how well you presume to know me."

To his own surprise, he found the renewed acid in her voice reassuring. He spoke slowly, that each word might penetrate her gloom. "You have taken pains to explain to me why your people are discontented. I may have been blind to the slights and misfortunes you feel so keenly, but one thing I do see clearly is how much these folk rely upon the grace and blessings you offer. I cannot allow you to dismiss what you are to them, not now when they most need you. So, by all means, let me rekindle your impatience with me if it will spare you from unhelpful doomsaying."

Selida's brows flattened over her eyes. He met her frown, and did not look away. "Aluna save me," she sighed, as she again began to climb the stairs. But this time, her voice was a touch lighter.

"She does," he agreed.

They stopped outside the moon- and tide-marked door. It felt too soon. Kahldar would have appreciated another flight or three, to see her self-possession more fully restored. He considered Ser Aegison's orders: to watch her, constantly. "I will see you inside and then retire to the barracks," he said at last. "Wait for me to come to you tomorrow morning, and we can return to the stables to check on your patient and her child."

She fished in her sleeve for the key. "You're not going to sleep in the hallway to make sure I do not send traitorous signals to our besiegers?"

It was uncanny, how often she seemed to read his silent thoughts. "Will you give me your word that you will not?"

"Would that make a difference?"

"It would. To me. And, I suspect, to you as well."

"Really."

"Yes."

She sighed. Loudly. "Then, to protect your reputation

with Ser Aegison, yes: I pledge by the Serpent of the Sea that I will not."

"Thank you. Though it is not my public reputation, but my personal honor that concerns me."

Before Kahldar could turn to go, she stepped into his path.

"Wait." Selida placed a hand on his pauldron. He could feel it... through the metal, through the leather, through the bandage and the ache of the wound underneath. "Show me your shoulder."

He dared not. "It... is late, and all your prayers are spent. Sergeant Finch can tend to such minor injuries well enough."

"I reopened your wound," she said. "This morning." He wondered if fatigue made her stubborn. *More* stubborn. "I should have remembered it, and insisted on healing you as soon as Lady Magnus mentioned it."

"I am glad you did not. Tonight's patients had far greater need of your goddess's healing."

Her shoulders set. "The least I can do is change your bindings. Take off your pauldrons, your mail, and your tunic, and I will see to it."

Temptation—to bask in her competence, to allow her to perform a task she clearly relished and preferred— dried his mouth. "Are you refusing to stay in the chapel unless I comply?"

She pushed him gently backwards into the little room until his knees hit a chair. Then she turned his torso so that his shoulder faced the altar, and lit a brace of candles to provide an even light.

"Sit," she said. "I will do the rest."

Kahldar could feel her fingers undoing the leather straps. The weight lifted away as Selida removed his armor, piece by piece. Eventually, he sat before her in breeches and boots and the soaked-through bandage.

"The wound is not deep," he said.

She cut the bandage free with a pair of small silver scissors. He winced as it pulled at the newly-forming scab. Her cool fingers soothed his burning skin, touching him this way and that. "It may yet take infection," she said, "but you are right, the cut was clean. Let me change the dressing and apply another bandage. Aluna willing, I can heal you in full tomorrow morning." A smile, lovely as evening jasmine, touched her lips. "It's not like I won't know where to find you."

Her fingers returned to his skin, and then came the rasping sting of a cold cloth. He felt very aware of his relative nakedness, of the allure of her body so close to his. All she would need to do was look down, to see the evidence of it. "This is unseemly."

"Seemliness matters only when you're not bleeding," she said. "Here. Rest your forehead against this other chair, and relax."

He had intended to close his eyes for just a moment, but when he opened them again it was to the sound of her settling into the chair beside him. The room was dark, and the door to the hallway closed. He still wore his boots and breeches, and his wounded shoulder tingled with cool salve under its fresh new bandage.

Selida had snuffed all the candles save the ones in her bedside alcove, and a latticed screen muted these to a soft glow. The open window over the altar let in moonlight. After the close air of the birthing stall, the fresh silence caressed his skin like a balm.

She placed her hand over his, where it rested on his knee. Kahldar marveled at the way the faint celestial rays lined her fingers in radiance.

"It seems neither of us is getting enough sleep," she said.

His eyes followed the moonlight up her arm, past her shoulder, and to her cheek. She had pulled the clips out of her hair, and it wreathed her face in sinuous waves. Her pupils were huge and dark.

With incredible effort, he rose to his feet. His shoulder throbbed, but the pain was drowned out by his awareness of her: her scent, her skin. Selida's hand was still in his, so he pulled her up beside him.

"Thank you. I... should dress, and return to the barracks."

Her free hand touched the naked skin of his waist, sending lances of heat through his body. "You don't have to go." She stepped so close he could feel her warmth through her robe. "What better way to ensure I am up to no mischief than to stay the night?" His vision pounded as her fingers splayed against his abdomen, and he imagined them drifting lower.

"You offer more than I can accept." He captured her errant hands, and returned both to her.

Her lips quirked. "Because you have paid no bride price?" Selida reached up to cup his cheek. Her thumb traced the edge of his mouth. Kahldar felt his lips tingle with awareness. "You cannot buy what I would offer: myself, and a moment to be alive together." She leaned in further, so that her lips brushed the corner of his mouth. "What is mine to give, I would share freely with you tonight."

Her other hand was tracing lines of fire on his flank, above his pelvis. His skin became a battleground, awash with ambushes. He could not think. If he shook his head, his lips would touch hers, and then he would kiss her... and then, he knew, he would not be able to stop.

Kahldar took a shaking breath. "I told you last year. I took a vow. I cannot."

Her lips hovered beside his ear, and her breath sighed through him. "Do you still hold yourself apart for some Welded bride who may never appear? Whose name you do not even know?"

"That does not matter." It took incredible effort to say it — even to think it. "In the unlikely event that my liege someday chooses a wife for me, I would go to her with my honor untainted."

"Untainted?" Selida's voice squeaked upwards over the word, like an explorer over a surprise patch of ice. Her maddening caresses stilled. "You think I would *soil* you?"

He knew he had hurt her feelings, knew it was somehow both the truth and exactly the wrong thing to say. He also dared not delay. "Please stop," he breathed.

Her hands fell away and she stepped back from him. His skin mourned all the places she was not. He looked into her face. The aqua rings in her eyes were thin around wide pupils, but, as he watched, her mouth firmed into a small, ironic smile. "As you wish," she said. "Aluna smiles on passion, but a serpent will still scar the hand that grabs its tail."

He took a deep breath. "My shirt and tunic, if you will."

Selida took a step back from him. "I might taint your tunic." Brittle frost had returned to her voice, and this time it cut him deeply to know that he had put it there.

He tried to summon wit enough to explain. Eventually, he ground out: "I may live among your people, but I am a Dawnlander still. Exoeras showed us how to live in harmony, and we aspire to follow Their example. A man shows his respect for the future he and his bride will build together by remaining chaste until marriage. It is a tradition I am not sorry to uphold."

She glanced down. "Your body says otherwise."

Kahldar flushed, but refused to lower his gaze from hers. "I am more than my body."

She took another step back, hands spread. "We must all live by our principles, I suppose. I find the thought of binding myself in wedlock to a Dawnlander family unspeakably horrifying. I could never trade a lifetime of servitude for a night's pleasure, as enjoyable as you might prove to be."

It should not have stung, but it did. "And I hold my honor as dearly as you do your independence."

She tore her gaze away to fix on the window, and the moon beyond. "I am going to bed. You may dress and see yourself out, Ser Kahldar."

He gathered his garments and departed before the pain in her voice could make him reconsider.

Selida woke the next morning, finished her prayers, and opened the chapel door. She almost hoped to find the hallway piled high with obstructive furniture—an assortment of hazardously stacked weapon racks, perhaps, or a crenellated wall of wine barrels. Instead, she saw Kahldar, crisp and glossy and clad in plate armor. She would never have guessed he still harbored an injury had she not tended to it herself. He stood in an easy half-attention, filling the hallway as thoroughly as her imagined barricade. The scent of his soap in the warm air told her he'd been there for at least an hour.

She glowered at him. "What a clear conscience you must have, to idle all morning outside a closed door."

"But my conscience is not clear." He bowed, his expression both blank and grave. "Lady Selida. Allow me to apologize for giving offense last night."

Her heart skipped a beat in dismay. She fought to remain in her safe, petty sulk. "Then you retract your decision? I suffer rejection very rarely—and very poorly, it seems."

She'd hoped to provoke another blush, but his time in the hallway had apparently been spent in earnest philosophical contemplation. "I cannot. But I wish to clarify that my repugnance applies solely to the actions I might myself take at your invitation, rather than to yourself or that which you offered me."

Selida gave in and rubbed her face. It was either that or slam the door, and she didn't want the sound to carry to any petitioners who might be hiding below the stairs. "And you do not think that expressing disgust at the prospect of spending a night together might be, in itself, insulting?"

"Again, I am sorry for having offended you. But it was the fear of betraying my own expectations for myself that repulsed me." He paused, and this time she did have the satisfaction of feeling the air around him grow warmer. "I understand that your offer was intended as a gracious gift. I... regret it is not in my power to accept. To do so would be to forsake my vows, leaving me unworthy of your gift and of yourself."

He bowed again, and Selida forced herself to count to five as she watched the morning light halo his regret-colored hair. When her voice was steady, she reached out and touched his pauldron. "Let me heal your shoulder."

He rose and nodded, eyes steady. "My thanks. We also have time to go to the stables before breakfast, if you would like to look in on your patient and her child."

Selida closed her eyes, and summoned Aluna's blessings. *Knit him and keep him,* her heart whispered, under the cover of the usual words. *Safe from injury, pain, and above all, treachery. Above all, Tidemother, keep him safe from that.*

Selida pressed her face into Dulcis's warm neck. The mare whickered and nudged her elbow.

"I know," Selida murmured. "Humans are eating all your oats." Fishing around in her satchel, she produced a fat, stubby carrot liberated from the pile of stew ingredients she'd blessed that morning.

Dulcis lipped up the treat, crunching it with obvious satisfaction. "Shh," Selida whispered. "Ispen might get jealous." She glanced up, over the partition. Kahldar's broad back was visible in the adjoining stall, where he worked over his own horse's coat.

Kahldar did not turn. "Ispen will remain on three-quarters rations like the rest of Wyvernsvow's defenders." And then, in a gentler voice: "You seem fatigued. Shall I return you to Lady Magnus's solar?"

Selida resisted the urge to rub her eyes. Three days had passed since Ser Kahldar's apology, and, like two stiff-armed marionettes, they had fumbled their way into a tentative routine.

Kahldar now came to her door at dawn. Together, they made their rounds: she, blessing the families camped in the great hall, and he, collecting reports from guardsmen rotating through their duties. Then they paused in the kitchen, where her prayers bolstered the day's meals. After breakfast, she conducted services—sacraments in her chapel or Aluna's weekly mass—before he left her with Emmeline so he could take Lord Lydris to the practice yards. After dinner they walked the parapets. He counted watchfires on the ridge, straining to see them through the fog. She worried over the ships accumulating invisibly on the horizon.

None of the Fox's men had dared another assault over the wall, at least. Ser Aegison had likewise offered no reply to the Fox's initial missive, not even to return their remaining prisoner. "He's saving 'im in case we need to trade 'im for goods," Kahldar's sergeant confided.

They ended their evening walks at the cistern, where Selida devoted most of her remaining prayers to augmenting their supply of fresh water. Then Kahldar left her at the chapel door, extracting anew her solemn word that she would remain there until morning.

Alone at last in her bedroll, Selida teased Lydris's coin with divinations: *Where, in the great heap of caves under Wyvernsvow, did you once lie? Where might I find your kin?*

Aluna offered nothing but silence in reply.

On the third day, Kahldar had suggested that they

visit their mounts. She wondered if he could tell how the endless scrutiny wore at her composure.

"For the sake of convenience, I moved your steed to the stall beside Ispen."

Selida inhaled. Knights' chargers commanded spacious stalls, with windows that let in plenty of fresh air. Their stables were not shared with the families of farmers or fishermen.

Dulcis had greeted her with unflappable good cheer. Selida was afraid she would drape herself over her mount's back and weep. Instead, she had set to currying.

"So this is where you are," came young Lord Lydris's clear voice. Beside him, Selida could hear the sluggish slither of Emmeline's dress on the straw-strewn floor.

Selida lifted her head from Dulcis's coat. Lydris already wore his padded gambeson. He stopped outside her stall door, jumping from foot to foot, practice sword in hand. Ispen, more sensitive to noise than Dulcis, snorted.

"Here, my lord." Selida reached into her satchel and offered him the second carrot she had secreted there. "This one is for Ispen."

His face lit up, and he leaned against the adjoining stall door. "Ser Kahldar, is it time for practice yet?" He looked up at his mother. "Lady Selida can stay with you, can't she, Mama?"

Kahldar released Ispen's head, letting the giant horse reach for the carrot with extended lips. "Once I am finished here."

Lydris wriggled as Ispen's tongue licked his palm for more. "Will you show me the Leaping Ferret Strike? Or how about the Falcon's Pass?"

Selida watched Kahldar absorb this enthusiasm with the mute gravity of a sea sponge. "Given the current situation, Ser Aegison thinks you and the pages should put in a day or three of archery."

"Must we? Archery is so boring. What if you showed me *after*?"

"Perhaps, if you succeed in beating your previous record of four bullseyes." Kahldar gave Ispen a last, fond pat and stepped out of the stall.

"Off you go," Emmeline said, standing by Dulcis's stall door. "We shall return to the solar, and our embroidery."

"Oh, and Lady Cleric," Lydris said, stepping around his mother and into the lee of his hero, "I've sent a letter to our allies, informing them of the gravity of our situation. Have you had any luck with the coin I lent you?"

It sat heavy in her inner pocket. Selida dipped him a curtsey. "I'm afraid it is merely a coin, though the Church's historians will appreciate its role in our history."

"Oh."

"Perhaps the other objects housed nearby will prove more forthcoming," she heard herself say. "In my divinations, I did see a large, rune-covered pearl. Aluna's ancient clerics used them to store messages and communicate across great distances."

This riveted his attention. "Communicate to where?"

Selida spread her hands. "Scholars believe that in the time of our Elven ancestors, such pearls could reach all the way across the sea."

Emmeline placed a hand on her son's shoulder. "Lydris, you will be late and Ser Kahldar will be held to account." She glanced at Selida. "Unless, Lady Cleric, you would enjoy proceeding to the bailey to watch the pages practice?"

"None of the *other* pages have their mothers there," Lydris exclaimed, all indignation.

Emmeline pursed her lips. "Perhaps another time."

Lydris bowed hastily to them both before he and his knight clattered out of the stable.

T he stalls felt empty after Kahldar's departure. Selida kissed Dulcis farewell before following Emmeline through the courtyard and up three flights of stairs. When they arrived at her solar, Emmeline settled onto a padded bench. Beyond the large windows stretched the sea: moody, slate, and ever-changing. "Come, sit. You can tell me how the castle fares."

Selida remained standing. "I have never been well suited to embroidery and gossip."

Emmeline bit off a thread. "Perhaps you *would* have preferred we go watch the pages spar with their stalwart instructor." She smiled into the fabric. "He is a patient and exacting master. They love him dearly, though they would never say it to his face."

Selida had seen the way the young men shone when Kahldar spoke to them, the way they sought his opinion regarding their mounts, their gear, their stances. She dared not admit it. "Doesn't Ser Aegison wish to oversee your son's training personally?"

"Before all this unpleasantness, he did. It shows him off to his best."

"Really."

Emmeline arranged her embroidery hoop in her lap and set a perfect stitch. Contemplating the bouquet of flowers forming in its center, she said, "I know you do not like him much, but steadfast loyalty to a liege of six is a rare quality in a retainer. He demands more of Lydris than any other training partner, though Ser Kahldar has more patience."

"Dawnlanders." Selida sighed and stared out the window. Inbound fog obscured the horizon. "Do you never miss swordplay? What if we snuck off to practice, the way we used to?"

"And batter at each other with what, spindles? One of the best aspects of marriage was that I could finally let someone else worry about the business of bludgeoning and stabbing."

"As a travelling cleric, I cannot afford to delegate away activities that may yet save my life."

Emmeline leveled her a look. "And yet you stir up thoughts of pearls in a six-year-old child?"

Selida winced. "You say nobody is allowed to see the treasure, and I concede the point. But if there is some great power Lydris could call upon, locked away in his very own castle, should he not know? At least of the possibility?"

"Pray do not distract him, or yourself. The situation is tenuous enough as it is."

Selida sighed. "As milady commands."

Emmeline started on another flower. "So, how have you and Ser Kahldar been getting along?"

Aluna save me. Dutifully, Selida began to recount their recent exploits.

On the fifth day of Selida's incarceration, she and Kahldar once again climbed the stairs to Lady Magnus's solar. They found nothing but silence. "But they were at breakfast," Selida said, bemused, as she took in the rows of embroidery floss snug in their baskets.

Kahldar, even more accustomed to Emmeline's tranquil rituals, looked equally blank. "Perhaps we missed them."

Retracing their steps revealed no sign of either Lydris or Emmeline. They passed through the kitchens, the larder, and the length of the great hall. Farmer and fishing families greeted them from their temporary living spaces along walls and corridors, but no bright blond head bobbed among them.

"Lord Lydris?" said one of the pages tending the horses. "He hasn't yet come down for practice. Why do you ask?"

Selida felt the air around Kahldar congeal as he scanned the exterior walls. "Perhaps Ser Aegison is taking a turn at his education," she murmured as the page, dismissed, scampered off.

"Far more likely he would have returned the boy and his mother to us posthaste." Kahldar's voice was even, but in it Selida could hear the scenarios that tumbled through his imagination: Some covert kidnapping? An accidental fall? A purposeful *shove* from a terrible height? He looked up at the towers. "We must search systematically, from top to bottom."

She hurried to catch up. "You're not going to involve Ser Aegison?"

"If the Fox sees our men in disarray upon the walls, he will know his plan has succeeded."

Selida wanted to shake him. "The Fox wants the treasure, not a child of six." *Aluna, what would he even* do *with him?*

The treasure. She saw the caves then, the gnarled grottoes and endless, black corridors. *What time was it?* The tide was already high. Ice flooded her stomach.

"Oh," she said. Taking in her expression, Kahldar pivoted abruptly on his heel.

Well, Tidemother. I suppose this is one *answer to my* prayers. The thought was black, jagged, and brittle. *Surely not.*

Side by side, they raced back towards the larders.

ELEVEN

The breathless maid found them in the hallway outside the kitchens. "Ser Kahldar!" she cried. "Lady Magnus bids you attend her in the lower reaches."

Selida saw Kahldar swallow a curse. "Is he hurt?"

The girl looked pale and confused—infected by Emmeline's urgency without knowing whence it came. "Who? My lady caught me outside the blacksmith."

"Go to the barracks and tell Ser Aegison where we have gone," Kahldar commanded.

Selida caught his shoulder. "Don't charge through the kitchens. You'll start a panic. I'll go first."

His expression flattened, but he let her precede him into the dense space.

"Lady Magnus passed this way not a quarter hour ago," Dame Pottage said. "Is aught amiss?"

"Oh, yes, she asked us to come attend her," Selida said

as she eased Ser Kahldar through the minuet of scullery maids. "We'll be but a moment. Don't disturb yourselves."

Once they had ducked into the first of the larders and passed the tunnels Ser Aegison had designated as the castle gaol, Kahldar broke into a jog. "They'll certainly be disturbed when Ser Aegison arrives," he said.

"Then we'd better return before that. I don't want dinner on my conscience in addition to everything else."

He shot her a glare. "In addition to what else, exactly?"

Rolling her eyes, Selida flung her arms wide, as if to indicate the caves, the castle, the very Tidelands. "All of this, obviously." Gritting her teeth, she shoved Lydris's credulous eyes out of her mind and ran onward.

S elida had last visited Wyvernsvow's deepest caves when she was a girl. Their scent—salt and the grot of tidepools—resurrected a memory of her brother Laurence, once Lydris's age. He had plunged into the damp warrens, determined to find a secret passage connecting the keep to the beach. *"We'll surprise all those Dawnlander lords."* When she'd hesitated, he'd added: *"Imagine how proud father will be."*

Lord Coralglass had pulled them out before they'd managed to drown in the flooding, twisted passages. *"You won't unite the Tidelands if you're dead."* He'd lifted Laurence by the scruff of his tunic and shaken him like an errant pup. Then he'd turned his scowl on her where she sat dripping and bedraggled, knees and hands dashed open by the stones. *"And you, snakelet, where was your good sense? Your mother didn't buy his life with her own just for you to let him drown."*

Now, as Selida followed Kahldar through the upper reaches of the maze of caves, she whispered a prayer for the dead, the one that transformed ghosts back into memories. As the words passed her lips, she imagined folding their images into the tiny driftwood box she wore on her girdle. *Such a little box, for so very many ghosts.*

Kahldar halted at the end of a corridor cluttered with empty racks for drying fish. When he turned, the torch he'd retrieved from a wall sconce exaggerated the severity of his features. "After this point, you must cover your eyes."

Selida pursed her lips. "Surely you jest."

"I do not. Even before Lord Lydris discovered the treasure, only he, myself, Ser Aegison, and Lady Magnus were allowed beyond this passage."

"For security?" She and Laurence had not discovered a passage to the beach, but perhaps others had.

"Yes."

She blinked. *Confirmation?*

"But also to spare you the temptation of any familiarity with the caves. If you thought you knew how to navigate them, you might try to return."

"You *do* know that my brother and I played here when we were little."

"I... did not. But it has been many years, and the sea has likely changed them."

"Lady Magnus's need sounded urgent."

"Aye, but I must insist," he said. "Or I will entrust you to Ser Aegison, and return here alone." He cocked his head, frowning. "I can hear the tide already. The lower passages are certainly flooded."

"You are wearing armor."

"Which I can remove if necessary. Fortunately, I've learned to swim."

She stared at him. He was as inevitable as the dawn. "Fine. Shall I close my eyes, or will merely pretending to close them be enough for you?"

Kahldar ignored her sarcasm. "Hold the torch."

Selida took it, pointing it well away from their bodies. Stepping closer, he drew the turquoise stole from her shoulders. It was voluminous enough to encircle her head twice over. When he reached around to tie off the ends behind her, she smelled heat and metal and sunlight, even in these depths embraced by earth and ocean. Though she could feel the urgency in his fingertips, he avoided catching her hair in the knot.

"You realize that if I cannot see our path and you slip on some seaweed and dash your head on a rock, we'll likely both drown down here."

Catching her gesticulating hand in his mailed fist, he placed it on his waist. The metal slowly began to warm under her skin.

"There," he said, reclaiming the torch. "Are you ready?"

Selida took a cautious step. "You also did not bother to ask if a cleric's stole can be used as a blindfold." For extra security, she pressed her free hand to the other side of his chestplate. She could squeeze all she wanted, and he would never feel a thing. "Perhaps such blasphemy will curse you."

"If that were true, I trust you would have said so ere I finished. Now, watch your step. As you said, the ground is slippery."

They had taken two right turns and one left in the span of a hundred and fifty steps when Selida's ears caught a whisper of prayer. Releasing Kahldar, she jerked the stole down away from her eyes.

It was Emmeline. She was pale, taut, and dressed in only a soaked lawn shift. Her clothes and shoes sat in a neat heap beside a second, guttering torch. She knelt at the edge of a growing pool of black water. The moist walls pressed them close. From the shadows on the rock, Selida guessed that high tide would half-submerge this place.

Kahldar had already averted his eyes. "My lady—"

"What happened?" Selida grabbed the kirtle off the pile and tried to swaddle it around Emmeline's shoulders.

The other woman did not let her. Pushing the kirtle aside, Emmeline wrapped icy fingers around Selida's wrists.

Through her shivers she managed: "Good. She f-found you. Th-thank Aluna y-you've come." She turned her head to stare at the black water. "As s-soon as I r-realized he was m-missing, I came, but c-could not follow." Her eyes reflected black. "Find him, s-save him, and I will f-forgive you the s-stupidity of p-planting this th-thought in his m-mind."

Selida found her cleric's voice: the cool, soothing one, the one Aluna gave her to give in turn to mothers who grieved their children, and children who grieved their mothers. "Slow down, Emmeline. Where should we look?"

"I remember the route to the treasure," Kahldar said, stripping off gloves and plate. "How long has Lord Lydris been missing?"

Emmeline convulsed, her body one knotted mass of will and tension, helpless in the face of mortality. "He t-told me after b-breakfast he h-had a s-special p-practice. Archery. I d-didn't think to look for him until after noon."

"And by then the tide was coming in," Kahldar said.

Selida felt her stomach flood with vinegar. "Is it still reachable?"

"There are pockets of air in the caves even when the water is at its highest," Kahldar said. Breastplate, pauldrons, and gorget rang as they hit the floor. "The treasure lies under one of them. If he is there, I will bring him back."

Emmeline shoved Selida away. "G-go with him."

"Selida must stay with you," Kahldar told her softly. "I will go."

Emmeline turned her black eyes on him, and Selida saw him flinch. "Take her," Emmeline said, wrapping her arms around her slim torso. "Aluna w-will not l-let my son drown."

Selida inhaled. Aluna took many things. Everything, in the end. She imagined the energetic blond head disappearing into the depths, stilled by cold and blackness. Drawing a deep breath, she took off her shoes. The black, slimy sand squelched between her toes, quickly numbing them.

Kahldar had stripped to his undershirt and chausses. He reached for but did not quite touch her shoulder. "Lady Cleric. Stay with Lady Magnus. I will return shortly."

"She m-must go with you," Emmeline said, her voice as frigid as the sea. "I command it."

"If Lydris is injured, Aluna will heal him," Selida said. "And I can breathe underwater."

Kahldar's mouth was a flat line as he lowered himself into the thigh-deep pool. "Fine." He held out a hand to her. "Hold on, and do not let go."

"Shall I share air with you?"

He looked impatient to be off. "No."

The stab of annoyance elicited by his flat refusal was a welcome reprieve from her other thoughts. "Serpents of the air, Aluna bids you fill my lungs," she exhaled in the old tongue. Then she inhaled—in, and in, and in.

So he had *learned to swim.* They waded into the icy black. Selida grabbed his shoulders as he stepped off a shelf and plunged into the briny water. The cold swallowed her like a serpent enveloping its prey. *Tidemother, take us and hold us.*

Kahldar sank down, down, down, his weight dragging her after him. When she opened her eyes, stinging against the salt, she could already see the torchlight receding as the rough walls closed in. She set her teeth to endure, and let him draw them both into the darkness below.

CHAPTER

TWELVE

They'd been under for too long. The twisting caverns deflected the worst of the tide's pull, but it still tugged them back and forth as the ocean gushed into and out of the passages. Kahldar swam with power, but slowly, to avoid scraping against sharp rocks or straying into dead ends.

Selida could still feel his fingers, strong on her wrist. After diving past half a dozen crevices, he kicked upwards, towards the ceiling. She felt hesitation tighten the muscles on his back: the tide must have erased a pocket of air he had been counting on. She mouthed a prayer, and a slice of waning moon, barely visible in the pitch blackness, coalesced between them.

Kahldar's face blurred into view against the backdrop of pitted stone. Selida gestured at the narrow cave around them. *Does that help?*

He glanced down towards another passage, but hesitated again. Selida saw his eyes dart back the way they had come, weighing his remaining air against the need to press forward.

Finally, after a last frustrated glance around, he started to pull her towards the tunnels leading back to Emmeline.

Oh for Aluna's sake. Before he realized what she meant to do, Selida twisted under his arm and came up hard against his chest. He was new to swimming, while the ocean had been her childhood playground. Pressing both palms into his torso, she kicked off a wall. Her momentum carried them both back against the rock as she used her grip on his shirt to press her lips to his.

She felt his dense body stiffen, felt his hands close around her shoulders to shove her away. Before he could, Selida reached up with one hand to pinch his nose shut. Cradling the back of his head with her other hand, she sealed her mouth against his. Then, she opened her throat and exhaled Aluna's air into him.

He jerked under her, and by the shared magic of her prayer his involuntary gasp became a deep inhalation into already-full lungs. Their garments floated like jellyfish between them as he stilled in surprise. Selida continued to exhale. She counted the seconds to herself: *One. Two.* His palm came up, just enough to graze her cheek. *Three.* Slowly, she closed her lips and pushed herself away. His fingers trailed through her hair, undoing some of her coils from their loops.

They floated there, in the trace moonlight, as his lungs

struggled to make sense of his new reservoir of breath. Selida, watching him, felt the tide tug every surface of their bodies, moving them through the dark like partners in an ancient, elemental dance.

The images came to her involuntarily: sliding herself up once more against him, tangling her fingers in his hair, wrapping her legs around his waist.

Kahldar was watching her, mouth closed, eyes dark. *Who would you be,* she wondered, *if you were free of your Dawnlander oaths?* A different man, she supposed.

Turning her head, she gestured down at the crevasse he had glanced at. *Shall we?*

Kahldar nodded before touching his chest with a questioning expression.

Three minutes, she signed.

This time, instead of taking her hand, he drew her along his back. As he wrapped her arms around his chest, the tide fit them together like a pair of nesting spoons. Then he dove, driving them further into the tangled depths beneath the castle.

S elida understood, now, why she and Laurence had never found the treasure. Hoping to locate an outlet to the beach, they had searched ever downwards. Kahldar, however, now turned upwards, past turns too convoluted to remember. *How* had *young Lydris come all this way? Had Aluna called to him?*

Long after a mere human breath would have run out,

she saw her first glint of gold: a coin lodged between two shadowed barnacles. Moments later, she saw another, and then a pair, both bearing Aluna's visage. Just beyond lay a pearl brooch, the sort her parents might have brought and offered here to beseech their Goddess to smile on the birth of their second child... had the temple not been destroyed by Dawnlanders the year before he was conceived.

Another sparkle caught her eye—the clasp of a small metal chest, ivory engraved with pearl—and then Kahldar rounded a corner and Selida would have cried out, if she dared spare the air. Spilling down around a pillar of dead coral, her little light illuminated a veritable dragon's hoard. Gold coins formed a lavish bed for precious stones, chased goblets, silver platters, and delicate altar figurines. Stalagmites grew throughout, and small fish flitted among the stone teeth, their glinting scales a living mirror of the treasure below.

It was beautiful in a way that made her chest hurt: a fillip of the once-great wealth of the Tidelands, gifted in exultation and sorrow to their Goddess in years gone by. Each jewel, a joyful thanksgiving; every coin, a fervent prayer.

Which of these yearnings did You deign to grant, Tidemother?

Years of funeral boats, released silently to the sea, piled up in her mind. *Aluna grants all prayers,* she had counseled grieving fathers, mothers, and children. *Just not always in the way we ask.*

The chill in her heart returned. *Tidemother, in what way do You intend for me to grant our people's prayers this day?* The implications of these riches stretched out before her: armies and bugles, and castles rebuilt over ruins. *Surely You cannot find greater value in this child's passing than in his seal-pup smile.* Despite the wet black surrounding them, her skin felt hot, and then cold, and then hot again.

Selida reached out to a gold bust of the Goddess, half buried in sand. *Meet my eyes and tell me that this cannot be what You want.*

Kahldar seized her hand in an iron grip. Pressing it back against his chest, he pointed urgently into the darkness.

Past the treasure, in the far recesses of the cave, she saw a larger movement. The long sinewy tail of a coldfire eel fluttered against a wall. Where there was one, Selida knew, there was usually a nest. And they were very fond of metals.

Then, she felt Kahldar stiffen. A moment later, he surged upwards towards something floating at the edge of a shelf which jutted out from the wall.

It was Lydris. Breaking the surface of the water, Selida exhaled blessed air and sucked in the familiar, dank scent of the tidepools. The boy slumped as if asleep, his body half submerged in the surf.

Kahldar heaved himself onto the ledge, his hands reaching to measure breath and pulse. Selida floated behind him, suspended in cold possibilities.

"Still alive," Kahldar declared, his voice hoarse. "Exoeras, we were close." Then he shook the child by the shoulder. "My lord? My lord, you must wake up now."

Selida hauled herself to the lip of the shelf, the weight of her clothes and hair dragging her backwards. "Wait. He's not sleeping. Look." There, under Lydris's hand, sat an enormous pearl. At least the size of her palm, it was shaped like the inside of the clam it had once inconvenienced. Ancient script sparkled and slithered over its surface. As she watched, its glow seemed to match the ebb and flow of the water in the cave. Her stomach knotted, and she had to remind herself to keep breathing.

"Is he ensorcelled?"

Selida's mouth felt clumsy as her heart began to surge. "Those are runes of memory and language. He might be... communicating with someone."

Kahldar's face contorted. "How do we wake him?"

"Let's break contact, first." Gently, she wrapped her fingers around Lydris's wrist. It was cold, the pulse thready. *Aluna keep you,* she mouthed, and a little bit of blush came back into his pale cheeks. Then she lifted his hand free.

The pearl leapt *up*, through the air and into her palm. Selida had not guessed it could do that, nor was the movement accompanied by light or scent or any of the trappings of magic. It was simply sitting on the rocky outcropping one moment, then rising into her outstretched hand the next. Its scarred surface touched her skin—

Selida was eighteen. She stood with chapped palms and aching knees before the Grand Cleric's driftwood door. She raised her hand to knock, but her movements were slow; the hallway was underwater. She glanced around, but her vision fractured as if she were looking through a kaleidoscope of sea glass. Around her coiled the prayer-worked stone warrens of the Grand Abbey, but through them she could also see the arching wall of a deep, dark, cool place: a grotto hidden in the womb of the ocean, always shadowed and yet writhing with life. The ghost of a great peace surrounded her, deep and intimate.

Tidemother?

She pushed open the door. It creaked and dissolved like a whisper worn thin with years. The study was dense with green-yellow light and the memory of a hymn. The Grand Cleric's chair sat beside her embroidered firescreen, and in it Selida felt the *absence* of an enormous presence. A faint warmth lingered in the hollow of Her dented cushions.

As she stared, trying to understand, her awareness fractured again. Though Selida was still standing in the Grand Cleric's office, she was also five, tracing the embroidery on her mother's cold pillow. She was seventeen, flushed and bewildered in the silent garden. She was twenty, dry-eyed, hands pressed to the fresh grave marker. She was the serpent, climbing the rise before Wyvernsvow with a heart full of lead.

Then—

"*S elida!*" Her eyes burst open as the last of Kahldar's bellow echoed through the flooded chamber. He had seized her by the shoulders and shaken her hard enough to jolt her head backwards on her neck. His grip burned through the cold fabric, scorching her skin.

He was so *present*, so utterly intent, that gratitude welled up behind her eyes like hot vinegar.

"It's just us." The words came out a strangled mumble.

His face contorted. "Selida, can you hear me?"

Her tongue sat enormous in her mouth, and her lawn shift was a slimy film over her skin. Her chest felt like an empty bottle, shriven through with cracks. She tried his name: "Kahldar?"

He leaned closer. "What was that?"

Her eyes must be dilated; she could see every ridge and crevice of the rock wall above them, writhing like scales sheathing coiled, lithe bodies. Beside her, the crescent moon she had conjured earlier shone like a star.

She tried a simpler word. "P-pearl?" She turned her head. Lydris, still limp on the rocks; the cavern, still close around them; the water, still nibbling at the rocky shelf; the treasure, still glinting like a fever dream beneath the black surface.

Kahldar shook her again, no more gently. The heat radiating off his body warmed her like a fire. "It— possessed you. You fell backwards and started to spasm. The pearl fell into your lap. I dared not touch it, so I heaved you over and it rolled," he glanced downwards, "back into the water."

Her limbs felt suffused with sleep, and reluctant to obey her. "It was Aluna's," she said. Her cheeks were hot. Her eyes smarted.

His lips writhed. "Did—did you see her? Talk to her?"

"No." Selida inhaled—delicately, so her chest wouldn't shatter. "It was more like... a memory. A vision of a place She once loved, but is no longer. It's not for... communicating." She looked over at where he'd indicated, but there was no sign of the pearl. "Or maybe it was... but no one is answering now."

She didn't realize the tears had spilled out of her eyes until his rough thumbs brushed them from her burning cheeks.

Her hands were too heavy to stop him.

Kahldar held her for a moment longer, as if afraid she'd dissolve like salt into the ocean if he let her go.

"Stay with me," he said.

"I'm here." Gingerly, she covered the back of his hand with hers. *The chair is empty.* She would not cling to his warmth. She must not. Forcing her fingers open, she turned her face away from his molten gaze.

With a rough exhalation that might have contained words, Kahldar shoved himself back onto his heels. Her eyes were still adjusting, and in the light of the crescent she could now see... well, all of him; the wet fabric hid nothing. She focused on the strong swell of his shoulder, under the snaking wetness of his hair. *The cave. Lydris.*

Emmeline. Right. She wiped her eyes and pulled her knees up towards her chest, as a courtesy to his modesty.

Kahldar returned to crouch over Lydris. The tide was still rising. He pulled the boy deeper onto the little shelf, so that his back rested against the rough wall. "He's getting colder." They both listened to the waves roaring in the distance. "We have to move. Can you pray more air into his lungs?"

Selida estimated the passages and hairpin turns in her head. "Only if he is conscious to accept the blessing." She inched forward until she could touch Lydris's wrist. His blood bumped erratically against her fingers. "If we cannot wake him, we will have to wait until the tide goes back out."

"That's hours from—" He took a breath and tried again in a quieter tone. "If Lord Lydris is missed, the castle will fall into a fatal disarray. If the Fox takes the keep—"

She could imagine what he imagined. "I'm not sure, but Lydris may well spend as much time unconscious as he did immersed in the vision." She scrubbed at her face. Salt burned the folds of her skin, her eyelids, her cuticles. She felt ten years older than she had this morning. "Let's try rubbing his hands and feet. It might rouse him faster."

Kahldar seated himself with his back facing her. "I'll take his hands."

THIRTEEN

"He won't stay warm," Kahldar said. He was still rubbing Lydris's fingers. The water was now lapping at their toes, cold and inexorable.

It felt like hours had passed in this close, damp dark, but Selida knew it had only been minutes. Her second healing prayer had sent a brief flush through the child's body, but it was gone now. His lips were faintly blue. "I know."

"The barnacles on the wall climb halfway to the ceiling. If, at highest tide, we must tread water and hold him—"

"I know."

"Can you conjure some sort of heat?"

"Not today." As patches of her shift began to dry, the lingering salt caused them to stiffen and chafe.

Under his breath, she heard him mutter, "My kingdom for a Welded Dawncaller."

She did not dignify this with a response.

Eventually, he spoke again. "I... don't suppose there's something in the treasure we could use to wake or warm him? If there were, would the lightning fish allow you to reach it?"

He must be desperate. And so was she, to not chide him for courting treason. Selida crawled to the edge and stared down into a tangle of discarded altarpieces. "I'm not afraid of the eels. But..." She paused. "Why *is* the treasure here?"

"Lydris thought it was an act of your goddess."

Selida looked upwards, her brain sloshing into motion. "Well, yes, but this isn't just some pirate's lost treasure. These cups and coins belonged to the temple that once stood atop these caves. The acolytes must have hidden their remaining wealth when they knew they would be overrun."

Kahldar picked up Lydris, cradling him in his arms to share more heat. "What of it?"

"Well—how did they get all of it *here*? It was heavy, and hard to carry. They wouldn't have had time to bring it through the caves. Certainly not along the route you followed." She scanned the walls and ceiling now, looking for scales and coils beneath the barnacles. "Didn't you notice that you led me first down, and then up?"

Kahldar frowned, attempting to follow her reasoning.

"Are… you suggesting there might be some passage connecting this cave to the main body of the keep?" He shook his head. "Impossible. Lord Magnus and his engineers would have discovered it when they were building the castle."

"It wouldn't look like a passage you could use. It would be a gently roiling surface, like—" Her eye spied a likely stretch, broad as a man's shoulders and covered in slime and barnacles. Underneath, the rock was coiled and scored, like a mass of ropes heaped on the deck of a ship. It was exactly like the patches she remembered in the Grand Abbey, and the one in her own father's keep.

A moment later, though, her enthusiasm chilled. Kahldar had made a good point, though not the one he'd intended. *A sister cleric surely gave her life to hold this treasure, and its route, secret. Who am I to betray her trust?* And then there were other, darker considerations. She glanced at Lydris: skin chalky, bright hair gone dark, too cold even to shiver. She heard the words in Laurence's voice: *What if this is what She intended? What if this is how he is meant to serve the Tidelands?*

Then why did She sweep him onto the shelf when She could have drowned him? Why did her knife-eels not burn him to death with their cold fire?

Laurence again, his sleepless eyes worn, his voice bitter: *Pearl or no, Her chair was empty. This is how we bring Her home to us.*

"Selida." Kahldar's voice dispersed the vision of her brother like a wind through bonfire smoke. He curved his body as if to protect the boy's with his own. "Selida, talk to me."

Her name, unadorned, drew her gaze to his. *He was here, though She was not.* Her aching heart made its decision between one beat and another.

"I need a finger of clay," she said, dropping to her knees. "Any will do." Her nails grated and chipped as she scrabbled in the divots of the gnarled rock beneath them.

Act before you think better of it.

"Like this?" His toes found a pocket of wet earth, as much sand as dirt.

She dug into it with her fingertips. *There.* Barely more than a handful of damp soil; just enough to squeeze into a rough cylinder between her palms.

Selida focused her attention on the swirling portion of the rock wall. It sat barely within reach of their little outcropping. Behind the slime, behind the barnacles, her fingers touched stone scales. Rising on her tiptoes, she pressed her hand against it.

When she could feel the enormity of the earth through her skin, she closed her eyes. The prayer boiled up her throat: "Aluna, wake Your servants of stone. Let them come to me as the ocean comes upon the shore." And then the unnecessary but even more heartfelt addendum: *Please let this be Your will.*

She felt her prayer drop into the intimate absence the pearl had shown her. Panic seized her breath. What if by *seeing,* by *doubting,* she'd sundered her connection—

Selida smashed the clay in her other palm flat, and the

rock under her hand exploded into a massive tangle of soft, cool bodies. They surged over her fingertips, seeking purchase. The ones who couldn't escape down her arm cascaded outwards along the walls. The sound of their scales and the hiss of their breath overwhelmed her senses. They streamed over her throat, her ears, her eyes. Selida staggered under the weight of them. Hundreds of serpents. Thousands? A river of snakes flooded over the bridge that was her body. Selida forced herself to be still, willing them to remain animate until every one was resting safely against the floor and walls, and her reaching hand touched only emptiness.

The air abruptly filled with the stench of imprisonment and infection. Torchlight spilled from the new tunnel, turning the backs of her closed eyelids crimson. Frantic cries echoed through the stone. Ser Aegison was not among them, but Selida knew he would arrive soon. *Thank You, Tidemother.*

Selida ungrit her teeth and opened her eyes.

On their side of the cave, a starburst of stone snakes wreathed a new, round hole in the rock. The sinuous bodies, now still, adorned the ceiling and walls like a baroque relief. On the ledge's surface, a matching halo of serpents ringed the spot on which she stood. *No mistaking what happened here.*

Given the ragged hysterics she could hear coming from the guardsmen, they had likely witnessed a matching explosion on their side of the opening she had created. *Serves them right.*

She turned her head towards Kahldar. "There. The castle dungeon. The passage is short enough for you to pass him through, with some help."

Kahldar was already on his feet, Lydris over one shoulder. His expression alternated between nausea and awe. But he drew a deep breath, composed himself, and called out to the guards beyond: "It is I, Kahldar, with my Lord Lydris. He is cold, wet, and ill. Fetch him a blanket and warm a bath immediately."

Then, turning back to Selida, he slowly sank to one knee. "Thank you, Lady Cleric. And thank Aluna on my behalf, for I see she walks in your footsteps."

Her lips parted, but she could not decide whether to rebuke him for blasphemy or, worse, accuracy. "You may relay that to Ser Aegison, when he arrives to bellow about this turn of events."

She could not tell if her words had registered, but his steady eyes caught and held her gaze. "She does," he repeated.

FOURTEEN

S ome hours later, Selida lay in Lydris's room, her pallet stretched across the floor at the foot of his bed. She could hear the deep, even breathing of a child in restful slumber. She timed her breaths to his in an attempt to drown out the cacophony of recriminations tumbling around inside her head.

First among these was her failure to secure Aluna's pearl while she had the chance. Ser Aegison had immediately thronged the new passage to the treasure room with his most trusted guards. Unless she found some means of turning herself invisible, there would be no way to retrieve the pearl now. And if she did—her heart quailed at the implications of the vision it had granted her. *Tide-mother, where are You?*

The second was Lydris's near-deadly misadventure. He'd awoken with some excitement after his hot bath, only to shrink from Emmeline's tautly restrained rage and relief. The conclusion of his hasty justification for the deception about the practice yard had not helped: "...but I found this pearl, just like Lady Selida said! It was as big as my face and showed me visions of the ocean. There were huge creatures and tiny ones, and Sea Elves, and songs, Mama! Songs from a thousand harps, pouring down like rain."

When his mother, unmoved, listed all the ways he might have died and thereby failed in his duty to his people, he had paled. Then he apologized and apologized until he fell asleep over his dinner of porridge and honey. This had left Emmeline with nothing to do but sigh intermittently and rest her portentous gaze on the woman responsible for inciting the whole affair.

Now, Selida could see Emmeline just beyond Lydris's bed drapes, again robed in black and ensconced in furs. She sat on the padded bench beside her son's headboard. Despite her fatigue, she was sewing, her needle passing into and out of the fabric with a fervor meant to ward against all that could have been.

Selida rolled over onto her back. If only some prayer, uttered with equal intensity, could shield her from the panic that had blindsided her after Lydris was put to bed. Once everyone was assembled and confident the boy was out of immediate danger, they'd had a tremendous row over the young lord's copper tub.

"And you told me nothing of this?" Ser Aegison's fists and moustaches had both trembled, though he was exerting obvious effort to keep his voice down. He glanced at the door to Lydris's bedchamber. "I could have gone to fetch him."

"Your place was on the wall," Emmeline had said, her usual warmth scraped thin. "Ser Kahldar and Lady Selida found him, and all is now well."

Ser Aegison had rounded on Selida. "You saw the route to the treasure?"

Selida, still stiff with salt, said, "I believe the original route is irrelevant now."

"Had she not been with me, Lord Lydris might have slipped into illness, or worse," Ser Kahldar attested.

Vindicated, Selida had glared at Ser Aegison. Then she blinked. Had Kahldar just taken her side in front of his commander?

"Aluna's clerics must have hidden their treasure by using the Tidemother's blessings to part and then seal the stone." Emmeline's slow words had trembled with equal parts exhaustion and wonder. "Only another cleric's prayer could have reopened the passage."

Ser Aegison's hand, gently resting on the copper which had cradled Lydris's head, moved to point at Selida. "So you're telling me a *prayer* burrowed through a six-foot rock wall? What other stone might she breach?"

Selida had glowered. "If I wanted to make the keep fall into the ocean, I clearly could have done so by now."

"Or perhaps you simply never had the opportunity." He'd looked at Kahldar. "Keep an eye on her at all times."

Kahldar remained expressionless. "We already do."

"*ALL. TIMES.* Sleep inside her door if you must!"

Selida's hot gaze met Kahldar's dark eyes for a fraction of a second—and, instead of his typical wooden reserve, she saw a new openness which terrified her. The vibration building in her heart rose in pitch until she felt her ribs might shatter. Visions assaulted her: the quiet chapel, a moonlit kiss, his defenses crumbling. Yet deep in her body, beyond reasoned thought, she knew this would end not in a simple, long-sought conquest, but in ruin.

Panicked, she had snapped, "For pity's sake, give us five minutes' peace of each other." And that was why Selida now lay on the floor of the boy's room, in easy reach should Lydris or Emmeline have need of anything.

It was almost midnight when Selida heard heavy footsteps pause outside in the hallway. Emmeline rose from her bench, crossed the room in a whisper of shadow, and opened the door a crack. Selida squeezed her eyes closed. If her unruly thoughts had somehow summoned Kahldar, she wanted to at least pretend to be asleep.

"I am sorry to disturb you," came Ser Aegison's voice. He sounded apologetic, almost courtly.

Oh, for a noose of kelp. Selida opened her eyes again.

"He is sleeping," Emmeline said. "I will speak with you outside."

From her position, Selida could see that Ser Aegison had found a washbasin and his best tunic. In

Wyvernsvow's teal and silver livery, he was nearly handsome.

"I—am not sure this is a conversation for a hallway."

"Yet I am afraid that is where we must have it."

The knight commander inhaled. Selida read his purpose in his flushed, abashed grimace a moment before he fell to one knee.

"Lady Magnus—Emmeline—I have long held my tongue about my feelings, hoping to bring my suit when your year of mourning had passed, but tonight, danger has made me reconsider."

"Ser Aegison—"

"Consider marrying me. I am the third son of a noble family. I have served your late husband faithfully since I was a page. Given the unrest brewing in the Tidelands, the King, I am sure, will bless our union."

Emmeline's voice was low, but even in this moment Selida heard how hard she strove to infuse her tone with kindness. "Do not do this, Garret."

"Think of the Tidelands, my lady, even if you are not inclined to think fondly of me. The people grow restless under the rule of a boy of six. Together, we will of course hold the land for him, until he reaches his majority, but should—Exoeras forbid—something happen to him, the people deserve a clear succession."

"Garret, you must never suggest such a thing. I will not have it."

"My lady, I am merely being reasonable. The Fox is only so bold because he knows that if he takes this castle he will revive the Tidelander resistance. Do not give him and people like him reason to target your son."

"Rise up, Ser Aegison." Emmeline stepped back from him, gently but firmly detaching her hands from his. "In my husband's memory, I beseech you: Never speak of this again."

Selida flowed silently to her feet in the canopy's shadow, in case Ser Aegison mistook Emmeline's empathy for uncertainty. But when he rose, his hands were as open as his expression. "I... must do as you command. But please, my lady. Consider it."

Stepping back into the room, Emmeline closed the door quietly in his face. She saw Selida standing behind the bed. Two bright red spots burned in her pale cheeks. "I'm sorry you had to hear that."

"I will pretend I heard nothing."

Emmeline went to Lydris's side, and brushed his bangs back from his forehead. "Garret is not a terrible man. Nor is it a terrible idea. But I could not do that to my husband's memory, or imperil my son in that way."

"Do you fear Ser Aegison would not hold to his word and preserve Wyvernsvow for Lydris? Or, worse, harm him if he had the motive to do so?"

"No. Ser Aegison is loyal. Blindly so, sometimes." Her voice was slow, thoughtful. "But were I ever to remarry, I would not put it past my new husband's family to prefer for their line to inherit, over Lydris's. So there will be no second wedding for me."

Selida pressed her fingers to her lips. "You prioritize

the safety of your child over the stability of the Tidelands."

Emmeline looked up, eyes sad. "They are one and the same."

"Believing so puts you at risk as well."

Her brows rose. "Will the Grand Cleric and the rebels prepare a knife in the dark for their princess if you tell them I said so?" A black smile touched the edge of her lips. "They might be surprised. They already sacrificed me once, yet here I still stand."

Selida spread her hands.

With both sorrow and sympathy, Emmeline asked, "Will it be *your* knife?"

"I pray not," Selida said, sitting back down on her pallet. "I have enough ghosts following me around."

Emmeline stepped around the bed and knelt at Selida's side. "If Lydris is the only hope for peace, then everyone, on all sides, must work to keep him alive. There will be no alternative."

Selida stared past her friend, up towards the ceiling. "Emmeline, I will protect you, and him, and all the people of the coast as long as Aluna grants me breath. But do not make me pick. Your insistence on this one, narrow path forward consigns many to years of suffering and suspense."

"If I compromise before I must, the world my husband and I foresaw will never come to pass."

Selida shook her head. "And I cannot stand by while our people starve, literally or in spirit."

Emmeline covered Selida's hands with her own. "Are you sure your life has been simpler, following the Church instead of following a husband? It seems the Grand Cleric asks quite difficult things of you, after all."

Selida squeezed Emmeline's hands back. "How shocked the girls we were would be to see us now. What is this womanhood of poisoned choices? Where are the violins, and the silks, and the dancing?"

"They will return. I see them, just on the horizon, even if you do not." Emmeline was silent for a long moment. "There is one other matter."

"Yes?"

"Is it true that Lydris saw a vision of Aluna?"

Selida felt her heart stutter. "I don't know."

"What did *you* see? I presume you took the pearl from him."

"It is still with the treasure." Selida swallowed. "When I touched it, I fell into some sort of fit. Ser Kahldar saw it drop into the water, and we did not retrieve it."

Emmeline's mouth pursed. "So you saw nothing?"

Selida considered lying. "I saw nothing that would give us a tactical advantage in this siege. If the pearl once allowed for communication, nobody on the other side is listening."

"And Aluna?"

"Is not waiting inside to guide us, not in any material way." She stared up at the ceiling. "It's just us."

"Ah." Emmeline's smile aged her a hundred years.

"The wisdom and power She pours through your hands must suffice, then."

"That does not stop me from wishing for more."

"Don't we all?"

"I know She loves the Tidelands, Emmeline. But what if none of *this*—" Selida gestured to encompass the keep, the siege, the whole of the world, "—matters to Her, so long as we return to Her in the end?"

"Then perhaps we need not fear being judged by Her for our mistakes." Emmeline sighed. "Speaking of which, I believe you owe both myself and Lydris an apology, for endangering him so. I understand why you did it, but you cannot keep looking into the past for solutions, Selida. You will break your own heart in the process, and everything else, besides."

Selida felt her eyes get hot. "I'm sorry." The memory of Lydris's gold hair, floating in the water, stabbed her through. "I should never have imperilled him for so little."

"I accept your apology. And I thank you for retrieving him, when I could not."

She had to work to get the words past the salt and the tightness in her throat. "Thank you, my lady."

"But, Selida. Don't be so foolish again."

She met Emmeline's eyes. "I won't." But it was Kahldar's face that she saw.

Emmeline was silent for a moment. "You must choose, every morning, which miracles you petition Aluna to grant. Do you always keep a prayer of stone shaping at the ready? Whatever do you do with it?"

In her mind's eye, Selida saw the arches of solid rock that held the back half of the keep suspended over the waves. With her mouth she said: "Strengthen bones. Seal mouse holes."

Emmeline smiled. "Ah; of course. The castle needs no extra drafts."

"It is cold enough already."

"Well, it is past time I bid you good night." Emmeline released her hands and began to rise. "Or shall I tuck you in?"

"Don't be so kind to me," Selida said, as she slid down into the pallet and turned her back on the warm room. "I cannot possibly accept."

Emmeline's footsteps returned to Lydris's side. "One can always be kind, Selida. Kindness is a lens through which to view the world, not a bag of grain one must ration."

Selida pressed her arm against her face in a futile attempt to stop the burning. "Wake me if you need anything."

FIFTEEN

"*May the serpents of the earth raise us up—*"

Selida was avoiding him. Standing just inside the chapel, Kahldar watched her face as she led knights, scullery maids, and fishermen through the songs and dances of Aluna's mass.

"*—as the snakes of the sky carry our hopes—*"

It was not his imagination. She kept her eyes fixed on the front half of the room. In the first row, Lady Magnus and Lydris clasped hands with the two little farmer girls from the road. Their mother beamed at them from behind.

"*—when the Great Wyrm floats our souls home—*"

Two days had passed since Lydris's rescue. On the first, Kahldar had offered to return Selida to her chapel and guard her door against Ser Aegison's suspicions. To his surprise, she had averted her eyes and insisted she stay close to Lydris's sickbed.

The next afternoon, when Lydris's usual enthusiasm had returned and Lady Magnus could keep him confined no longer, Selida accompanied them to breakfast but rejected his invitation to watch the boy's swordplay practice. She trailed Emmeline back into the castle like a living extension of the lady's long black veil.

The Fox, meanwhile, sent no more sorties. However, the campfires along the peninsula continued to proliferate, as did the dots on the ocean's horizon. Ser Aegison ran the defenders through twice-daily drills, but Kahldar knew he dared not push them too far. None could say when the Fox might finally make his move. The air grew heavy as both the keep and the skies awaited the coming storm.

Kahldar knew such moods inevitably led some men to carelessness, and others to zeal. After he and Ser Aegison had reported two disciplinary incidents to Lady Magnus at dinner, she'd announced an impromptu prayer service. "'Tis exactly what we need to ease our spirits. Selida?"

Selida had not looked up. "Of course, milady."

Now, Kahldar was surprised to see Squire Penson, with his still-broken nose, among the crowd in the chapel, along with the fellow who had been so impressed by the breakfast scones. Even more people stood in the hallway outside. Those who knew the responses chanted them, and those who did not looked regretful.

He touched the *W* embossed on a disk adorning his armor. Kahldar had been taught that the Tidelanders' religion, like that of many other pagan peoples, was not so much incorrect as incomplete. Unable to conceive of or comprehend the entirety of Era's glory, they worshipped a mere facet of Her divinity as a goddess unto itself: Aluna. Now that this truth had been recognized, it was only a matter of time before this sermon, and many others, would be replaced by the mass of the Church of the Heavens.

But, he mused, Era did not claim dominion over snakes… or scones.

Selida ended the ceremony, inviting those who wished for confession to remain. Her serene expression offered him no answers. So he weighed his words, and waited.

K ahldar was still standing by the little blue doorway when the last petitioner departed. He saw Selida's shoulders tense in silent dismissal. Ignoring this, he watched her resolutely keep her back turned towards him as she straightened chairs and neatened the simple altarpiece.

The voices of his village priest and priestess echoed in his mind: *Strength and wisdom beget honesty. Honest words beget harmony.* His heart accelerated. He cleared his throat.

"The people of the keep are grateful for your prayers," he offered.

She slowed her neatening, but did not respond.

"As am I. For the water. For the healing."

She walked to the altar, and knelt.

He took a deep breath. "Young Lydris would have died in the caves without your miracles. Thank you for insisting on accompanying me."

This earned him a sliver of her cheek.

When she said nothing, he pressed on: "I was mistaken in believing I could have found him, or saved him, on my own."

"Is that an apology?" Her voice was unreadable, but he felt it like a fresh breeze on his skin.

"It... yes. I am sorry I dismissed the help you offered in good faith."

She rose, and lit a bowl of incense on the altar. "It is the dark of the moon tonight. I have one more ritual to complete before I retire to Emmeline's room for the evening. You will not want to see it."

"Why is that?"

"It is a ritual of purification. A bathing ritual."

"Ah."

"It ought to be done in the ocean, but that seems unwise in this weather."

"Indeed." He studied the painted walls for a moment. "I would stay, if you will permit me."

Seconds passed. "You could ask Emmeline to come, if you prefer."

"I will face the wall, so as to preserve both of our modesties."

"Why?"

Closing the door, he placed a chair in front of it,

facing away from the room. "Because I suspect I have again offended you in some way." Seating himself, he regarded the portal's masonry frame. "If that is so, I would like to understand why, so that I may make amends."

Her voice sounded strained. "You have not offended me."

"Then why have you been avoiding me?"

He heard her moving chairs around. "Have I been?"

"Yes."

Her next answer was, he thought, too rushed to be entirely truthful. "I thought you might enjoy a respite from my company."

"On the contrary, I have missed it."

"Truly."

"Truly." Perfect sincerity parried her wary skepticism. "Before this siege, I did not rightly understand the role you play in the fabric of your people's lives. Now that I do, I admire it."

"Would that all Dawnlanders shared your sudden open-mindedness."

"It is an abrupt shift, I know. I regret my long inability to see your people clearly. Perhaps we actually cultivate such blindness... lest, in comprehending your ways, we lose our determination to convert you to our own." When she was silent again, he added, "Pray do not stab me in the back in a fit of pique."

"Do... you think I would?"

"No."

Her voice was dry. "You say that with the utmost faith. I am amazed."

"I do not think you would betray us. You may be angry with Ser Aegison, but you continue to refill the cisterns. You feed the hungry." He contemplated a *W* engraved on his gauntlet. "You understand duty, and uphold yours most faithfully."

He heard metal chime on stone, as if she placed a large bowl in the center of the room. Then followed the sound of water, perhaps from an ewer. Kahldar fixed his eyes even more firmly on the wall beside the door.

"Perhaps," she conceded. "But my ultimate duty is to Aluna, not some messy worldly authority."

"A worldly authority simplifies many things. Who to honor. When to kill, and what distinguishes warfare from murder." He looked down at his hands. "Why one ought not take up arms against one's family, even to reclaim one's own birthright."

The sound of pouring water paused. "I heard that yours was an old Dawnlander family," she said. "But I had assumed you were a second or third son."

"I was my father's heir, but my parents died to a northern raid when I was nine."

"I am sorry."

He did not bother to shrug. She had lost her mother even younger, he knew. "King Harald awarded my father's lands to my uncle, so they will now pass instead to his eldest."

"Is there anything you could have done about it?"

"Just as the sea and its plenty shape the Tidelands, mountain winters and the trolls they drive against our borders shape the Dawnlands. I could not have defended those lands and their people when I was a boy."

"But now?"

"My uncle is an honorable man, in his way. The people trust him, and he holds the hungry creatures at bay. Merchants cross our lands and furnish the people with all they need. When I reached my majority, King Harald called me to his court and honored me with his perspective on this matter. So, instead of contesting my uncle's appointment, I chose to serve elsewhere—first in the east, and now on the coast."

"And so," she finished thoughtfully, "became a man who follows."

"You say that so scornfully. Must all souls yearn to lead? So many beautiful songs can only be sung by a choir in harmony. And unwavering loyalty is much easier on the spirit than the endless gnawing of ambition."

"Does the lack of freedom not grate on you? Ser Aegison is a narrow man."

"He is dedicated to Lady Magnus and to our young lord," Kahldar said. "He makes mistakes, but his intent is praiseworthy. There is no dishonor in following one such as him."

She was silent for a moment. "Does young Lydris know that you fight for him to retain a birthright that you yourself could not?"

"That is not why I serve." He exhaled. "Though I suppose the thought may occur to him, someday."

"And what if Ser Aegison had asked you to torture his prisoners? Could you have done it?"

"I would have. But a Dawnland commander ought not order a sworn knight to dirty his hands on his superior's behalf unless he has no other option. Ser Aegison knows my opinions regarding torture. It would have been dishonorable of him to ask it of me."

"He knows your opinion on torture?"

"As he knows my thoughts on the merits of parlay." Kahldar opened his hand. "It is my duty to speak my mind when I believe him to be in the wrong. But not in public, before the eyes and ears of those who might mistake such words for insubordination."

"Ah. I had wondered." After a long moment, the pouring sound resumed. When she continued, the hint of a smile had crept back into her voice, warming his heart and his hopes. "You have a poetic turn of phrase, when nobody else is listening."

"A private indulgence."

"You enjoy the troubadours?"

"Some of their songs approach the beauty of Welded poetry. And you?"

"I resent the Welded teaching that only married individuals have the wisdom to provide divine counsel."

Letting this pass, he pressed, "And troubadours?"

He heard the clatter of rocks on the wooden floor, as if she arranged a spiral of smooth stones around the basin.

Beyond her room, the keep had quieted sufficiently to allow him to hear the sigh of fabric on skin. Kahldar closed his eyes. He would not imagine her robed only in the warmth of the candles. He would not imagine her breasts, creamy and soft, nor their rosy tips hardening in the cool air, as they had under her stole last year when she danced in the surf. He heard her garments slither to the floor.

"I suppose I find their tales of courtly love... aggravating."

Kahldar took a deep breath. Here it was. "I am... sorry to hear that. It would please me very much to admire you from afar. Since you did say that you would abhor a more permanent, traditional connection."

He waited for three whole breaths, more chilled and tense than he had been in the caves beneath the castle.

"Kahldar," she said at last, "are you *trying* to vex me?"

He caught the snowflake sliver of disappointment an instant before it could pierce his heart and break it open. Willing his voice to remain even, he deflected, "I've noticed you often do your best to vex me. I long wondered why you seem to derive such pleasure from it."

"And have you found an answer?"

"I've discovered I would rather you speak to me in exasperation than not at all," Kahldar admitted. "But still more would I prefer your esteem, even if my vows prevent me from accepting your body."

"Does it so upset your Welded order when a man and a woman join in honest appreciation of each other? Do your priestesses not possess prayers that delay childbirth to its appropriate season?"

He chose his words with care. "Prayers do not heal the heartaches inflicted by such fleeting joinings."

"Many of your Dawnland squires seem quite unconcerned by such hazards."

"Not all Welded youths keep their vows as I do. Perhaps their childhoods featured fewer inspirational examples. Or," he smiled ruefully to himself, "maybe they are insufficiently fond of romantic liturgy. Exoeras teaches us that combining the flesh merges the soul."

"Are you worried I've left a string of sundered souls all up and down the coast?"

"Ever since we met, I've assumed that half the bard-songs in the region were composed regarding you."

This time she laughed. "I am not fond of minstrels, and I try not to trifle with any heart that is not at least as guarded as my own." Her voice softened. "I am sorry that I... misjudged yours."

Kahldar did not want to respond to that. He took a deep breath. "Why are tales of courtly love not to your liking? Many women, in both our homelands, seem to find the idea of being worshipped from afar appealing."

The basin rocked against the stone, and he imagined her stepping into it. Little splashes, then, as if the water lapped at her skin. "Many women are lonely in their marriages, or long widowed. Some troubadours take advantage of that, making courtly professions and ingra-tiating themselves in such ladies' households. Not all, of course; some have true bardic talent, but I have learned to be suspicious."

"Ah." Kahldar wished this knowledge did more to dull the pain of her rejection. "Visiting minstrels seem to delight Lady Magnus, but I suppose she might now do well to cultivate such wariness. The proposals she has received have no doubt been different from your own."

Again the sound of water, cascading over limbs and back into the bath. "Yes and no. She was born a handful of years before myself. Two years after she wed, King Harald's messengers approached my father with a similar suitor for me."

"Was your father amenable to such a match?"

"Hardly. But we were in grave debt on account of your King's new laws. Through the Dawnlander's bride gift, my father might have preserved our lands for my brother."

"What... did you think of him? Your Dawnland suitor?"

"He was thirty years my senior, and had no sense of humor. I could not imagine moving to the mountains and reshaping myself to fit his expectations."

"Lady Magnus made it work, somehow."

"I do not have her long patience for politics, and I was my father's oldest child. The thought of giving up swordplay and split skirts to simper and pretend at peace was intolerable."

"Would you not have had to give them up anyway upon marrying a Tidelander nobleman? Or did you perhaps expect to lead a rebellion alongside your husband, Aluna's banner streaming from your lance?"

"Nothing so grand." A long pause. "At the time, I'm afraid I fancied myself in love with a minstrel."

He inhaled. "Ah."

"I thought we might run away together and travel the coast, as he alluded to nightly in his verse. However, he was dependent on my father's patronage, and at the critical moment he declined. I had 'misunderstood' him, he said. It turned out that, for a man in his position, courtly love was much more practical than the alternative."

Kahldar flinched. "I... see." He held his breath for a five count, as bitter disappointment gave way to sympathy for the girl she was, and ire for the man who had crushed her hopes as she had now crushed his. When he had mastered himself again, he asked, "Could you not then have accepted the marriage your father proffered?"

"I had arranged for us to be discovered together, which irrevocably solved the offer from the suitor. My father turned me out for disobedience, but I think it was my lack of foresight that he really could not abide. Luckily, my aunt had a place in the Church. She introduced me to Grand Cleric Ethedra, Tidemother keep her, who was able to weave a different tale around my actions."

"I... always thought your devotion to Aluna came from great piety."

"Oh yes. I am deeply grateful to the Goddess for saving me from a short life of disinheritance, banditry, disfigurement, and lurid public execution. It turns out that, nestled in such gratitude, a desperate sort of devotion can indeed take solid root."

"Only one of her chosen could have rescued Lydris from the caves." Grateful for the distraction from his own feelings, Kahldar focused on the memory. "When the snakes opened the passage, it was because you rang through with sincerity."

"As I must. If I did not, the miracles would not come." She splashed. "But, of course, you are right. I follow Aluna because She encourages me to make my own way." Her voice dropped. "Perhaps excessively so."

He was silent for a moment. "And—how did you recover from having chosen and loved the wrong man?"

He heard the water pouring again. He imagined her tipping the ewer over her crown, turning her hair into dark coils on her skin.

"If the Welded teach that such a thing would blight your soul permanently, then let me assure you that is not actually so."

"Heresy." But he was smiling, a little.

"I promise you, a catastrophic error of judgment is not so bad, if you've survived the making of it."

"If."

"If," she acknowledged. "There's certainly a period at the beginning when everything tastes like self-recrimination and the future looks as impossible as a becalmed sea. But if you survive all that, you wake up one morning, a year or more later, somehow desirous of a good buttered scone."

"That sounds agonizing. Even with the best of scones to console you."

"It can be." He heard another splashing sound, and then her skin on the stone as she stepped out of the basin. "The good news is that every mistake you outlive makes you much more likely to choose better, the next time."

"Is there any wisdom that could possibly make all that agony worthwhile? Anything it could have taught you that was worth the price?"

"I suppose... to find integrity attractive." She made a self-deprecating sound. "Though it seems that has its own pitfalls."

He heard the sound of her feet on the stone behind him, and saw a faint radiance, beyond that of the candle-light, reflected off the wall before him.

His pulse jumped. "Selida—"

"The ritual has left me with a small measure of Aluna's blessing to bestow," she said. "Rest easy. All I will touch is your shoulder."

"Selida, I—"

"Don't." She laid soft fingers on his pauldrons. Her voice sounded like broken glass. "You cannot give me what I ask without unravelling what I most admire about you, and—" She swallowed. "And I cannot accept either of the loves you offer without unmaking what I most admire in myself." She stopped. Started again. "But if I can see you safe and whole into some better future, with some better companion, then these blessings I offer with all my heart."

Words poured up into his mouth. He could not remember the last time it hurt to breathe, when Exoeras' teachings fell away like so many platitudes to reveal a wound that went on forever like a tunnel to the center of the earth. The day he had left the Dawnlands, perhaps, newly knighted and excruciatingly aware that he would never again see his childhood home, or return to clear his parents' graves.

But, obedient to her preferences, he held all of himself behind his teeth as she began to whisper a prayer. Where she touched, a sharp, cold seawater washed through him. Before he could grow numb, he heard the hiss of foam over sand, and the lines of the room leapt out in sharp relief. A sea breeze surprised him, dispersing a weariness he had not known he carried. His heart beat on.

"There," she said, breath rasping in her throat. "That should last through your rotation on the parapet. Now I will dress so you can return me to Emmeline's rooms. I do not want you to suffer the indignity of sleeping across my doorway, and it soothes her to know I am there should Lydris have some unlikely relapse."

Finding words felt like threading a path through jagged coral. Without turning, he said, "Thank you. Though I mourn our differences, it is good to know how much we are alike. Your words are an intimacy I will cherish always."

Her voice was quiet, like that of a soul already moored upon a distant shore. "For what it is worth, I will treasure yours every day I yet live."

CHAPTER
SIXTEEN

Selida did not sleep. She lay on the floor at the foot of Lydris's bed, knees curled to the gaping hole in her chest. Snippets of their conversation tumbled over her like hammers on a too-tight dulcimer.

Every now and then she schooled her thoughts towards guard rotations and prayers, only to have them scatter like seafoam. All she could see behind her closed eyelids was Kahldar's profile; all she could hear was his voice. She relived, many times, their conversation: their wounds, their scars, her fine words of dismissal. She breathed silently through her open mouth so she would not wake the sleeping child by murmuring what she might have said instead, and what dangerous roads such words might have conjured. When morning came at last, the world looked jumbled and wrong, a nightmare of a nightmare.

Emmeline arrived to prepare Lydris for the day. Selida

dragged so badly that Emmeline, herself distracted, finally lowered the boy's hairbrush. "Are you unwell?"

The thought of seeing Ser Kahldar at breakfast, moving with reassuring steadiness among his men, made her eyes burn.

"It is the weather," Selida lied. The light through the window was weak, gray, and sluggish. "I wish this storm would break."

"It feels like coldfire air," Emmeline concurred, releasing Lydris from the bench. "Aluna willing, it will ignite the Fox's banners and not the thatching upon our rooftops."

Selida need not have worried. The great hall bustled with strained farmers and fishermen, but was conspicuously empty of knights. "Where is Ser Kahldar?" she asked as she passed a dish of eggs and onions to Emmeline. "For that matter, where are half the guardsmen?"

"Out and about, I suppose."

Something in her tone made Selida turn her head. The chatelaine succeeded in ignoring her; the young lord did not.

"There are sappers under the castle!" Lydris blurted excitedly.

His mother frowned. "Hush. Where did you hear that?"

Lydris lowered his voice. "From the stablehands. I

went while you and Lady Selida were in the kitchens. They say it's why all the guardsmen are on the wall." The boy smashed his eggs into a flat layer with the back of his spoon. "Do you suppose they'll dig their way up into the great hall, Lady Selida?"

Emmeline removed his spoon, and laid it beside his plate. "Nonsense. There are miles of cave under the castle, and good hard rock in abundance. Stop playing with your food; we must wait for Lady Selida to say grace before we can begin."

Selida found her voice at last. "Sappers?" she asked. "The Fox has sappers?"

Emmeline made a shushing gesture with her hand. "I too was surprised to hear it. Ser Aegison believes that they have grown desperate. Their current tactics have no hope of breaching the battlements before the King's reinforcements arrive." She narrowed her eyes at Selida, and then her son. "Ser Aegison and his forces are attending to the matter. He was very clear he did not want talk of their engagement to panic our people. We must keep this to ourselves, understood?" She waited for Lydris's chastened nod, then looked out over the uneasy crowds and raised her voice to carry. "Lady Cleric, would you say the prayer, please?"

I n the end, as no enemy archers had been sighted since dawn, Emmeline left Lydris with Old Meg and accompanied Selida to the cistern herself. By the time they reached the roof of the keep, the gray clouds were low enough to swallow the tops of the flags.

"Pray do not walk so fast," Emmeline said. "It's a rare treat to be outside. Do you not wish to savor the fresh breeze off the sea?"

Selida pressed against the parapet, scanning for signs of the sappers. She saw them only as they passed before the road leading away from the peninsula: a flurry of men, horses, and mining equipment clustered in a field surrounded by a copse of trees.

"It's the first clear land before the castle," Emmeline said, when she noticed Selida craning her neck for a better view. "No doubt why they started their encampment there."

"Are Ser Aegison and his men planning to ride out to meet them?"

Emmeline smiled, but her warning glance indicated the guardsmen on the walls beside them. "Lady Cleric," she said in a low voice, "Ser Aegison would say that is hardly your concern."

Selida reluctantly lowered her voice to match. "That is a typical Dawnlander response to sappers, is it not?"

"Allowing your enemy to undermine your defenses is generally considered to be poor form."

"You must tell them not to go. The Fox is a Tidelander. Our people have no idea how to sap a castle like this. He's as like to bury himself alive as he is to make any progress."

"There you go again, with that 'our people.'" Emmeline shook her head. "If Ser Aegison thinks it best to ensure that the Fox does not destroy the keep my husband built, I will hardly gainsay him on the matter."

"You don't understand," Selida snapped, before she remembered to modulate her voice. She tried again: "Apologies, milady. It is just that I am *sure* this is a diversion. As his rains of arrows are. It is a pattern with the Fox."

Emmeline took her shoulders and leaned back to study her. "Do you really know our foe so well that you can predict his moves? His thinking? I beg you, Selida, do not make such pronouncements."

Selida wanted to grab Emmeline's shoulders in turn —and shake her. "With all due respect, milady, do you think your father or brothers would know how to sap a castle like this?"

"It hardly matters, as the men out there seem determined to." Emmeline tugged her back towards the stairs. "Shall we?"

Selida ungrit her teeth and held her ground. "Please, milady," she said. "Imagine you stand beside your father, as he plots an assault against a fortified point. Your family had excellent cavalry." She pointed out at the attackers. "What would Prince Skyfawn have done, if he knew that this castle's defenders were going to assault his camp in the middle of that field?"

Emmeline sighed, but released Selida. Laying a hand on the battlement, she stared out at the sappers' position, her eyes going distant with memory. A moment later, a furrow creased her brow. "Hide in the woods," she murmured eventually. "And, when the counterattack came, sweep in from the west."

"Tell that to Ser Aegison," Selida said. "I beg you. If he bears you—or his men—any love at all, he must listen."

Selida was pacing outside the guardhouse when Emmeline emerged. "He heard me out, but did not seem particularly deterred," she murmured.

Selida could not tell if the other woman felt disappointed or reassured; Emmeline herself honestly seemed not to know. Taking Selida's arm in hers, she pointed her towards the inner keep. "At any rate, he believes they have the situation well in hand."

"Perhaps I should talk to him."

"I do not think he wishes to speak with you right now, nor would your words aid the situation." Emmeline started her long glide across the bailey. "Come. Some time with our embroidery will calm your restive spirit."

At that moment, Selida spotted Kahldar emerging from the stables with half a dozen other men. Her heart jumped, only to fall in dismay when she saw they were all dressed for open combat. She disentangled her arm from Emmeline's, picked her split skirts off the floor, and walked as quickly as she could in his direction.

"Ser Kahldar," she called, as soon as she thought it would not come out an alarming shout. "A word with you, if I may."

He glanced up, saw her, and paused. A flick of his hand dismissed the others to a slight distance. For a moment his face lightened, but then shuttered itself tighter than before. It clearly hurt him to look at her; regret opened a dangerous void behind her feet. "Lady Cleric. Apologies; I am in the midst of a defensive operation."

She tried very hard to look humble. "Are you riding out to rout the sappers?"

"I am afraid I cannot discuss that with you."

She stared up at him. *Forget last night; believe me now.* "I am *certain* that the Fox does not know how to sap a castle. It is not in the tradition of the Tidelands to dig through caves like a badger in order to undermine fortifications. He is as like to bring down a tunnel on himself as he is to collapse your curtain wall."

He held up a hand to ease her concerns, but she talked through him.

"What Tidelanders do excel at is ambush from cover. The sappers' camp is shielded on three sides by forest. Do you ride there now? I am certain that if you do, you will be riding into a trap. Please send at least some part of your force into the copse to the west of your target, so you will not be flanked unawares."

She wished he were not so good at remaining expressionless. "What has convinced you of this?"

"My father was a Tidelander general. It is what he would have done."

Kahldar's lips parted. Before he could speak, though,

Selida heard Ser Aegison's voice bark from across the courtyard: "Ser Kahldar. Attend me."

Kahldar stepped away from her. He inclined his head: a dismissal. "Lady Cleric."

Ser Aegison was not so polite. Ignoring Emmeline's quelling gestures, he erupted from the guardhouse, face thunderous. "Slither back to your chapel, Cleric," he ordered. "Whisper no more false tactics to your betters."

Selida felt her jaw set. "Risk your own life if you must, but do not risk your lord's defenders."

She watched him increase his stride and draw back his mailed fist. She wondered if she could turn the gravel at his feet to mud as he swung. *If he was incapacitated—if the keep needed another person to marshall its forces—*

"Knight Commander," Kahldar said quietly, "there is a matter in the stables that requires your attention."

Ser Aegison's head turned.

"An urgent matter," Kahldar added. He glanced meaningfully at the farmers watching them from all sides.

Ser Aegison's florid face reddened further, but he managed to control himself and correct his trajectory.

Kahldar turned back to her. "My lady." Behind his gentle tone, his eyes flickered with emotions she could not read. "If our paths are indeed to diverge, then we must start as we mean to go on."

All her words died in her throat.

He bowed. She watched him disappear into the stables.

CHAPTER

SEVENTEEN

"It will be well," Emmeline soothed from beside her.

Selida had not heard her close the distance between them. She tried to speak but could not.

Young Lydris's face appeared in the door to the great hall, outpacing Old Meg by half the length of the keep.

"Mother!" he called. "Is there to be a sortie?"

Emmeline straightened. "Stay your enthusiasm." Her voice rang with absolute, loving firmness. Lydris froze like a puppy at the limit of its leash. Emmeline nodded to acknowledge the watching refugees, and then took Selida's elbow. "Come. Let us give Old Meg a much needed rest, and return to the solar."

Selida hesitated.

In the stables, Kahldar addressed Ser Aegison: some matter involving formations and armored barding.

Emmeline lowered her voice. "He is a Welded knight,

following his commander's orders. Not even were you his priestess could you countermand that." She tugged gently on Selida's arm. "You may give Lydris a lesson, if you prefer it to embroidery. It will keep you both safely occupied."

Selida felt numb all over. "You could countermand them."

"My dear, that is not my place."

She barely registered that Emmeline had turned their steps towards the apartments.

"Are you not their liege?"

"My Lydris taught me long ago that once you have appointed your stewards, you must allow them to make their own decisions."

Young Lydris joined them then, bouncing first on one foot, then the other. "Mother, I'm sorry. I saw them from the window and forgot to keep my voice level."

"It's alright, my love. Why don't you precede us upstairs, and pull out your holy figures? Lady Selida has promised to tell us stories of the Tidemother this afternoon."

Selida pulled against Emmeline's arm. "This is not just about Ser Kahldar. Are you willing to consign your son's fate to this foolish decision? The fate of the Tidelands?"

Emmeline shook her head and pressed onwards. "Do I choose to trust an earnest man devoted to my family? I do so every day, just as I choose to trust an earnest woman based on the strength of our friendship." Emmeline paused at the open kitchen door. At her words the staff sprang to prepare parcels of bread and dried meat for the defenders. Then she glided on to the laundry, where she instructed the maids to prepare fresh bandages and towels.

Selida waited until they were once again ascending the spiral stairwell. "This is different. It is not just any day —this moment may change everything."

Emmeline smiled down at the hem of her dress. "You have seen quite a lot of people, riding up and down the coast. But what you have witnessed is a series of moments, each standing alone: weddings, births, funerals. When you live in one place as I do, you see that it is not only the days you expect to change your life which have the power to do so. My Lydris perished in a hunting accident. There was great significance to his decision to ride out that day, but how could we have known? He had been hunting for years. That morning, the question of whether or not to go barely registered as a thought." Easing open the solar door, she gestured Selida inside.

Selida balked. "Emmeline, the trust you extend to Ser Aegison is different from that which your husband granted him. Lord Magnus was party to his decisions in a way you actively evade. If he were here today, his opinion alone may have persuaded Ser Aegison not to go. And if not, the threat of his countermand might have."

"But *would* he have countermanded him?" Emmeline settled into her bench beside the window, looking pensive. "I knew him best in all the world, and I truly cannot say."

Selida stared at Emmeline's tranquil profile and felt the floor of the keep tilt under her.

Tidemother, all I wanted was to free us both of obligation or expectation.

Aluna's chair was empty, so it was the Grand Cleric's tart voice she heard instead: *And he understood you well enough, didn't he?*

Selida felt something crumple in her chest.

This is my fault.

This is my fault... and if I do not learn to live with it, how will I possibly manage any of the rest that is yet to come?

No governess had ever successfully cajoled Selida into learning embroidery, so she sat on the rug with Lydris. From a painted box, he withdrew a collection of carved figures: knights on horses, Dawnland ladies, Tideland fishermen. Pirates and boats followed, alongside farmers and wagons and pairs of well-loved animals. And, of course, the statue of Aluna Herself: twice as tall as the mortals beside Her, standing barefoot on a bed of coiling serpents.

All the while, Selida followed the progress of the sortie with her ears. Men and horses gathered in the courtyard. The portcullis and drawbridge opened. A clatter of noise, and then an aching silence.

Lydris, listening just as closely, arrayed the wooden creatures in facing rows.

"Have Lady Selida tell you the story of Aluna and the fisherman," Emmeline instructed. And then: "Your figurines are for holy instruction, not playing battlefield."

Lydris looked guiltily up at Selida.

"I suspect that Aluna does not mind that we play at war, so long as we also remember how to play for peace," Selida said. "Come, give me the fox and the mermaid and the knight, and I will tell you how Aluna brokered peace between the people of the sea and the people of the land."

"The fox?" Emmeline's lips pursed.

"A clever creature, capable of mediation," Selida said.

"May I be the knight?" the boy asked.

Selida carefully did not think about Kahldar, clad in full plate, astride Ispen, cantering towards the woods. "Certainly." She handed the figure back to Lydris. "Tell me his name, and we can begin."

Beyond the lattice of her preaching, the silence stretched on. The air outside the keep thickened. As Selida wound her way through one story, and a second, and a third, she marked the time in her head. Just now, the horses would be at the base of the hill. Now, leaving the road to cut across the scrub to the clearing.

An hour passed. And then another.

Lydris bounced to his feet. "May I go find the pages for

practice? We did shields yesterday and Ser Kahldar said my form was excellent."

"I'm afraid you must stay here today," Emmeline said. "Ser Aegison and Ser Kahldar are both abroad; the lady cleric and I need you to attend us."

"Are they fighting yet?"

Selida imagined it: the clearing, the sappers. The counterattack.

"They will tell you the tale when they return."

"I wish I could have gone with them. They took Aaron and Tucker."

"Aaron and Tucker are both squires."

Young squires, Selida remembered. Aaron played the harp. Tucker's mother and sisters huddled in the keep below. *Aluna save them.* The Fox would take hostages for ransom, would he not? A mounted knight in full armor was worth at least a town's harvest. Surely he had not fallen so deep into either resentment or piracy that he had forgotten the basics of chivalric exchange.

Lydris beseeched Selida with his eyes. "What do you think is happening? Is Ser Aegison on the front line? Has he kept his force together, or divided it in two?"

"Two, I hope."

He pounced. "Why? Is that strategically better?"

"Why don't you patrol across the doorway," Emmeline suggested. "This conversation would be much better held with your knight commander."

"May I at least patrol the corridor?"

"Go no further than the stairs."

It was all Selida could do to remain behind in the room. She rose to her feet and began sorting Emmeline's embroidery floss.

"Don't fidget," Emmeline murmured into her stitches. "Expressing tranquility is as much an act of faith as is delivering a blessing."

"I will organize a prayer service for tonight," Selida decided, still on her feet. "I'm sure the refugees worry over the departure of half their guardsmen, and will want something to occupy their minds."

"You will do no such thing. The keep will remain in readiness for the moment the men return. Sit and pray for them, if you please."

Selida sat. Outside the window, the invisible sun sank behind the wall of clouds piled atop the ocean. She could hear the remaining guardsmen making uneasy conversation as they changed shifts.

"I should be in the kitchen, helping to prepare dinner."

Emmeline smiled at her. "I remember your father complaining to mine that you had worn out three nursemaids."

Selida glowered at her and began Aluna's Litany of Wisdom, out loud and in Old Elven. With any luck, it would last them through dinner.

CHAPTER

EIGHTEEN

When distant shouts at last sounded from the outer courtyard, Selida was through the door, down the stairs, and across the inner bailey as if swept there by storm currents. "Slow down," Emmeline called from somewhere behind her, sweet voice chiding. "If I did not know better, I would think you awaited a lover's return."

Selida ungrit her teeth, turning so that her voice would carry back the way she had come. "No love could possibly be worth this much frustration." She winced as her words echoed against the stones. "I merely wish to see Ser Aegison's sour face when he is forced to admit that I was correct."

Emmeline came into view. "No, Lydris," she was saying, hauling on the young boy's arm, "you must walk —*walk*—with me."

Then her gaze slid past and, as Selida watched, Emmeline's placid amusement drained into a slow, ashen crumbling—eyebrows rising, lips parting.

The bottom dropped out of Selida's stomach. She whipped around. Men had filled the courtyard by the guardhouse, disorganized horses blowing hard.

Kahldar's voice carried clearly to her: "—close the portcullis. Raise the drawbridge. Archers to the south wall. Ready the oil; there will be ladders. Aim the arbalests at the shore; reinforcements are coming from their ships. This is a full counterattack!"

Beside her, Emmeline hoisted her struggling son into her arms. Her face had set, her lovely eyes gone hard. "I will barricade our people into the larders, to leave the kitchen and hall free for whatever needs the soldiers may have."

Selida's heart beat in her throat. "Will you—"

"I will. Go see to our defenders."

Selida was among them in a moment. Her practiced eye counted their numbers, comparing the ones who had gone out to the ones now returned. A dozen or more of their original complement were missing. The man who had lost an eye she touched with Aluna's blessing. Though it did not restore his sight, nor interrupt his shudders, it at least put a stop to the horrendous bleeding. She sent the man with the broken arm to await her in the chapel.

A stablehand swiped at the reins of Ser Aegison's horse, which squealed and pranced and snapped at all who came near. It still bore its grisly load, and Selida saw at last what Emmeline had known the moment the cavalcade entered the castle. Ser Aegison had tied himself into the saddle, but based on the splinters of spear protruding from the gaping hole in his side, she guessed he had bled to death not long after they had left the clearing. His horse's sides gleamed crimson, as if barded.

As she stared, Kahldar stepped inside the circle of the beast's flashing hooves. He grabbed the reins away from the stableboy before the horse could haul the lad off his feet. Kahldar forced the destrier's head down, breathing deep into its nostrils. It came to a shuddering, gasping halt beside him, foam from its mouth falling onto the ground to mingle with Ser Aegison's blood. Selida saw Kahldar close his eyes for a moment, mouthing silent Welded words of prayer.

Then he straightened. "Cut him down and lay out his body." The stablehand leapt to obey. Kahldar glanced down at Selida, and she saw that his eyes were empty of all but the need to impose order on the present moment. "Lady Cleric, please fetch your supplies and await us at the guardhouse. The men will have need of your skill before dawn."

"Kahldar—"

For a bare moment his expression softened, before closing again into a mask of efficiency. "Later," he said firmly. She took it into her heart like a promise.

A bugle of alarm sounded on the parapet. Selida ran for the chapel.

Kahldar did not see the enormous mace until it flared with inner light. It arced like a comet into his vision, the goliath wielding it soaring up over the edge of the wall as if Aluna had given him wings.

It was now past midnight. Spatterings of intermittent rain slicked the parapet. They had repelled the first two waves of attackers, while their arbalests forced the reinforcements to dock further down the peninsula. The bulk of his guardsmen had fallen back to take a breather. Selida had been among them earlier, dragging away the most wounded. He'd ordered her back to the chapel as soon as he'd heard her say that all her prayers were spent.

Then a new wave of ladders had appeared. Kahldar and three of the squires managed to shove two Tideland knights off the first of them. He had heard a shout and turned his head and then—

The blow landed. The angle was particularly unlucky. His breastplate crumpled. The squires screamed warning, too late.

His chest imploded into spears of fire—and fused. He landed hard on his back, sparks flying through his vision, and could not draw breath. The squires staggered back from him.

He heard *her* voice then—*Why had she returned?*— heard her scream his name—and suddenly every archer on the wall was screaming too as adders swarmed out of their quivers. Through a numbing black, he saw the snakes hurl themselves at his attacker. The mace went over the wall, the man shortly afterwards. His own men hauled him back out of the fray.

A rough ceiling: the sentry post.

"I don't care. Cut it off if you have to," Kahldar heard Selida bark at a squire. His dented breastplate clattered to the side, exposing his mangled chest and chain.

"Lady, do you need—"

"No," she snarled. Her face came into his vision: flushed skin, hair falling down in blood-matted coils. Then the burning agony in his body transformed into an ice so sharp he would have cried out, if his chest were not already shattered and useless. The cold retreated as suddenly as it had come, washing out of him with a fizzing sensation that left his lungs prickling with pins and needles.

"Find him a replacement cuirass," she ordered over his shoulder. "I don't care whose." Then, with shocking strength, she heaved him over and he was coughing blood onto the stone floor. Still dazed, he gulped in air. His lungs felt itchy, wet, and full of splinters. His ribs were iron lacework. He struggled to regain his feet.

Selida shoved him back down. "*You*. Don't you dare stand up until that child arrives with your new armor."

"Selida," he breathed, "I must. The wall... is falling."

The page returned, and when she slammed the new cuirass over his bloodied mail, her eyes burned with unshed tears.

"Fine," she snapped. "But: By the Law of Salvage, your life now belongs to Aluna." She leaned close. "Don't. Die."

NINETEEN

The hours wore on into morning, but the sky refused to lighten. It was nearly noon when the clouds finally opened. Sleet, shot through with lightning, stabbed down at the wall. Defenders and attackers alike scrambled for cover, and soon Kahldar heard the Fox's trumpeters call for a retreat.

From a sentry post, Kahldar watched water pour off the helmets of the withdrawing Tidelander knights. He took a deep breath. "Carry the wounded to the great hall, and the dead to the courtyard," he ordered the men waiting behind him. "Skeleton watch: Sound the alert the moment they return."

Once the keep was secure, Kahldar found Lady Magnus, Lord Lydris, and the refugees in the larders. They dismantled their barricade, and he praised the young lord for his readiness to protect his mother and his people.

Then he gave and received oaths, a blur of words almost drowned out by the roar of rain on the roof.

After that came more watches and shifts. Buckets materialized to catch leaks. The level in the cistern rose and fell as maids carried water off to boil for bandages. Kahldar marked time by the hollow lilt of the funeral service Selida sang up and down the great hall to ease the passing of her people from this world into the ocean's mysteries. The survivors' tears joined the raindrops' endless procession into the unfathomable deeps.

It was midnight before Kahldar was finally alone. His footsteps slowed, then paused in the doorway leading from the barracks into the bailey. He took one slow breath, and then another. The rain had come to a fitful stop after dinner. Through wispy clouds, he could see Era's new sickle moon, white in the sky above him.

His eyes drifted to where his thoughts had been all day: towards the corner of the keep that hid Selida's chapel. He imagined her there now, mixing salves to replenish her depleted collection.

Under his borrowed cuirass and mangled mail, his tunic was stiff from blood—and worse. His chest still tingled.

"Knight Commander?"

The title was as unfamiliar and ill-fitting as his new breastplate, and for the thousandth time that day he mourned the man from whom he had so recently inherited both. Inhaling deeply, he turned. "Report."

"Knight Commander, the guards have received rations of dried meats, fresh bread, and potatoes." The squire he had assigned to the kitchens was gray with exhaustion. "Your further orders?"

"Get some sleep, Aaron." As the boy bowed and ducked around him, he stepped out of the doorway and into the bailey.

The curve of her face. The anguished vibration of her voice. The sand-colored silk of her coiled hair. She had haunted and animated his thoughts all through the wretched mummery of this interminable day. *What does tomorrow bring?*

He could not imagine.

Instead, he saw the curl of stairs that led to her hallway; saw himself standing outside the blue chapel door.

There is no point. Nothing has changed.

Nothing had changed... except himself.

Kahldar closed his eyes, took a breath, and held it inside his remade chest.

Exoeras forgive me.

Vows were meant to guard the heart, just as armor did the body. Last night he had been stripped of both, and though his chest and shoulders chafed under their new coverings, his soul wished for even so makeshift a replacement.

The truth will have to suffice.

Terrified, he turned his steps towards Aluna's chapel.

Selida didn't realize she'd spent the past hours listening for Kahldar's tread in the hallway until she heard it. Immediately she turned, leaving the herbs half-ground in the mortar.

He did not look exhausted so much as drained empty. Her heart twisted at the bloodless cast to his fine features. Gore blotched his borrowed plate and mail. The garrison sergeant had bandaged Kahldar's arm, but she judged the hitch in his step arose more from the memory of his shattered sternum than any present injury. Aluna could heal the body, but the mind, as Her clerics often lamented, was beyond Her gift.

He looked at her like she was the only real thing in the world.

"Come here," Selida managed. She caught his hands, closed the door, and drew him into the room.

He took but a single step before halting. Wordlessly, she pulled his fingertips to her lips. He had taken a moment to wash his hands and remove the dried blood and grit from under his fingernails. *Chivalrous, to the last.* She pressed his burning palms to her cool cheeks and held them there until his fingers stopped trembling.

He spoke first. "You are no longer angry with me?"

"I was never angry with you." Her voice was hoarse. "I know none of this is what you wanted. For what it is worth, I am sorry."

Kahldar took one step closer to her, until the tips of his boots brushed the toes of her slippers. Leaning down, he inhaled through her hair.

"I am sorry, too. We lost much this day… but I am blessed and humbled to be standing here now." His eyes searched hers, drinking her in. "Since I rode out, all I have wanted was to see you again."

Selida closed her eyes. "Kahldar. Your vow."

He shifted, and she felt him brush his lips against her forehead. His breath was hot. "You claimed it. And myself. For Aluna."

Her throat closed.

"You should know—" His voice caught, and he started again. "You should know that this morning—before the counterattack—when we reached the stand of trees, the Fox's men did indeed attack from the west. Because of your warning, we were not taken completely unawares. Ser Aegison led our countercharge. Those of us who survived did so thanks to your counsel."

The words erupted from inside her chest. "I should have gone with you."

She felt his cheek graze hers. His breath tickled her ear.

"Even if you had been there, there was little more you could have done."

"I disagree. You saw, on the parapet, what I can do when I am at your side."

"I saw." He pulled back, just enough so that he could meet her eyes and press her hands to his armored chest, right over his heart. "Even so, I could only excuse your presence there because, if the wall fell, you would be in equally dire circumstances… and with only fishermen and farmers to guard you." He took a breath. "I could not imagine risking you in a sortie."

She frowned and leaned closer. "You will not order me away from you again. I am not the sort of woman who can stay behind while those I love ride forth. Yesterday, I thought I would go mad waiting for you. Not for all the serpents in the sky will I suffer that again."

She did not hear her own words until she saw his eyes widen, and his lips part.

Take them back, a voice inside her cried. *Deny them; beg him to unhear them. Ask it of him, and chivalry will forbid him from ever speaking of this again.*

"Selida," he whispered softly, reverently. "All that I am is yours. Body. Honor. Soul."

She could not inhale. His words stole air her lungs would never replace. Tonight of all nights, the memory of his heart's blood still on her hands, she could not prevent her body from leaning closer, her loneliness from accepting his warmth.

Don't do this, the voice begged. *Don't make every day to come a metronome of anguish from which neither of you will ever recover.*

His hands tightened around hers and the ground tilted away. Her heart spasmed, helpless. Terror engulfed her, as unfiltered as the night she'd found the garden empty, and all her hopes and futures suddenly blank.

Except... Kahldar was here. Stood here. Had come here. To her. And if she wanted him, she knew—beyond logic and reason—that he would always be here. Always.

"Selida," he said again. He tilted his head to kiss her.

"Tidemother save us," she whispered.

TWENTY

Kahldar had intended his kiss to be chaste, a grazing of his lips over hers. Selida's skin was cool and luminous: pearl and ivory and silk, treasures he would be appalled to sully with the filth still matting his armor and skin. He had not anticipated how his nerves would come alight in a tingling, confusing rush. He was not sure what to do when her tongue darted out to touch his... when she returned open-mouthed kisses to his nuzzles... when she captured, and bit, his lower lip.

He grew light-headed and, when she released his hands so she could wrap her arms around his neck, it seemed the most natural thing in the world to take her face between his palms, hold her firmly, and kiss her back. The low moan she made in the back of her throat as she arched up against him set his body throbbing.

As he kissed her, she pressed him backwards, step by

step, until the fire warmed his back. "Sit," she ordered, and he felt her hands on his shoulders, pushing him into a chair. He opened his eyes to look up at her. Her hair was coming undone from its serpentine coils, and her eyes were a ravenous black.

"May I—" Her voice was raw, as if she fought some invisible, inward battle. "May I remove your armor?"

Electricity shot through his body. "If you do, I do not think you will stop at my armor."

She stepped closer, between his open knees. Possessive fingers tangled in his hair as she leaned down to mingle her breath with his. "No. Unless..." The air around them filled with invisible wounds as her voice dropped in register with each successive word: "Unless you... still... don't... want."

He turned his face into her palm, smelled the salt of her skin. When his stubble rasped her wrist, she shivered; when his tongue darted out to taste her palm, he heard her swallow a groan. He opened his eyes and looked up at her flushed skin, her intense brow.

"I... want you. All of you." It might have been the truest thing he'd ever said.

She read his face. "But?"

His words choked in his throat. "I worry that, if I give you my body, you will break my heart and leave my soul in pieces..."

Expressions convulsed her features.

"...but I also worry that, if I do not, I will spend the rest of my life hollow with regret."

He saw her eyes fill, and she leaned down over him, jaw fierce, lips lush. "You will feel—no—such—thing." At the growl in her voice, he tightened with need. She kissed him, and he could feel the ghost of her fury from the parapet alive in her body. She kissed him again, once, twice, three times, further robbing him of sense. "I will not let that happen."

Her fingers unravelled his buckles; his helped. His heart beat like Ispen's hooves at full gallop.

"How?"

Her words were a torrent of raw silk on his face, his neck, every part her breath could reach. "I will mark you with my mouth." His pauldrons dropped to the painted floor, as she climbed into his lap to attack the straps that closed his cuirass around his torso. "Loneliness cannot cross the runes my teeth will leave on your skin." The pressure of her thigh against his made his fingers clumsy with urgency. "I will ravish you of thought altogether."

He gave up on the buckles and pressed his lips to her throat. She was salt and citrus and cinnamon. The dying firelight haloed her hair in its soft red glow.

"You are too shocking," he breathed, and nipped her.

She shuddered, and redoubled her efforts. Chestplate and backplate fell open like the petals of a flower. Together they wrestled him out of his mail, greaves, and boots. When only fabric remained between them, he caught her hard against his chest. Her body was taut, her breasts soft and yielding. The contrast overwhelmed him.

Her hands, one fierce around his neck, and the other reaching boldly below, made him gasp.

"I will touch you *thus*—"

He could not help it. He buried his face in her neck to muffle a moan.

"And *thus*—"

"*Selida*—"

"And if you are helpless," she interrupted, expression dangerous, "so too will be the regrets that seek to devour you."

He let her pull him deeper into the room, towards the bedroll hidden in the alcove; let her press him down into cool sheets that smelled of her skin.

"Selida," he managed. Her body came over his. She pressed down everywhere, as if she could shield him from the world. "Let me touch you."

She did something that made him arch up into her. He panted for air.

"Please—" He didn't know the words. Poetry fled as he reached for it. "I want—to please you."

"You do please me." He felt the brand of her mouth on his stomach; felt the shirt inching upwards to reveal the fresh scars that seared his chest. "And you shall. Now, and later, when I take you into me."

"Selida—" Her tongue and teeth turned his thoughts to molten glass. "I—give—myself—to you—"

"Kahldar—" Her voice broke as if gratification and grief were two shades of the same color. "You'll see. It doesn't work unless we give ourselves to each other."

Then she slid up his body and pressed him down into the bedding with mouth, breath, and brittle ferocity.

With a groan, he sank into the inevitable, like an exhausted and shipwrecked swimmer into the storm. He followed her mouth and hands, kisses and caresses, until all his thoughts were lost to an exquisite spiral of need.

He came back to himself for only a moment, and it was because she paused where she was poised above him, their slick flesh a delirious promise between them.

"Selida," he panted. She was luminous, intent, transfixed, transfixing. He wondered if she expected him to beg. Nothing, at this point, would seem unreasonable.

"I want to remember you," she said instead. "All of you."

"But... why? I'll be here."

Her dilated eyes filmed. A tear scorched his cheek as she leaned down to kiss him. An instant later, he felt her body seal tight around him and then slide home. Reason fled. Thoughts evaporated. He pulled her as close as two bodies could be, and let her show him all that she had promised.

And at the end, as her wet silk moved hard over him, he heard her gasp his name, over and over again, possessive and protective. Her face fixed as she chased her pleasure and spilled it back over them both. He heard her muffled wail—shock and relief—as she covered her face with her hands and convulsed hard around him.

It was too much. As deeply as he wanted to walk this edge a moment longer, his body succumbed to a bliss that overwhelmed thought, reason, and sense. Pleasure shredded him to pieces as he emptied himself into her.

Time yawned around them, the moment a droplet of honey stretching from the lip of a spoon.

Oh. Her prophecy had come to pass. The space between and inside them indeed contained nothing but silence, and worthy stillness. Outside the fortress of this moment, terrors and impossibilities yet crouched, waiting, but they were powerless before his certainty that *this*, at last, was right.

Between one breath and another, two bodies and souls become one. It was a very Exoeran scripture. He hoped Aluna would not mind.

Kahldar pulled Selida against him, and turned them so they lay nestled in the blankets. She brought his knuckles to her lips, and kissed him hard. *Strange.* Did she not already know she was irrevocably imprinted over everything he was, and would yet become? Before he could tell her this, or even douse the candles, sleep pulled him into a deep and dreamless peace.

CHAPTER
TWENTY-ONE

Selida came awake all at once. Her eyes opened to the guttering of the last candle by the altar. In its dying flickers, she saw what her body already knew: that Kahldar slept deeply. He fit perfectly against her—his face tucked into the hollow of her neck, his hands cupping her hips, his skin a radiant comfort against her full breasts. Sleep stole the wary judgment from his face, leaving its beautiful lines clean.

Goddess. She'd told him she loved him. No matter how she examined the words, she couldn't make them untrue. Worse yet, she'd promised to protect his heart from regret. *Reckless. Thoughtless. Foolish.* Her mouth flooded with dismay. The candle flared one more time before its glow dimmed, shrouding them in darkness.

Selida felt as if her heart was full of sparrows, scattering into the air before the methodical serpents of her thoughts could chase them down. She had been waiting for this moment—had she not? The door and the silent hallway beyond beckoned. She imagined it: tucking the pillows against his body, so he would not wake. Donning her robes and dashing barefoot across the cold floor. Pulling on her shoes only as she reached the hallway, and had eased the blue door shut behind her.

Traversing the keep would pose no difficulty. Every defender was gray with exhaustion. She could make her way above the postern gate. A thought would call a snake to deliver her message to the Fox. Then she'd wait until she heard her brother's familiar warbling whistle: an obnoxious robin awake before the sun. Obedient serpents of air would hold the sleepless knight below in helpless calm. She'd unbar the door.

And then—her imagination stuttered. Would Laurence keep the promise he'd made to the Grand Cleric: to bring just a few men, sneak peacefully through the castle, and take only as much of the treasure as he could carry? Or would her kinsmen thirst for revenge after long weeks of nothing and their fruitless assaults on the walls? She imagined hard hands closing over her. She imagined being made to watch as they ran rampant through the wounded. Those pirate ships did not belong to knights. They might—

No. Laurence would not let them.

He would take her hand like he had done when she had seen him off at the pier all those years ago. He would grin, and invite her to follow him.

This time she would accept.

She would lead him down beneath the keep, past the dwindling stores. They would free his imprisoned man, disable the guards stationed around the serpent-wreathed gateway, and perch on the ledges of the black cave. She would lull the electric eels to sleep. Then her brother's men would open their enchanted purses and disappear the treasure into them. She would tuck Aluna's singing pearl into her robes, to investigate at her leisure.

And then—and then they would leave the way they had come. She would follow, riding pillion, because there was no way to free Dulcis from the stables without raising suspicion. And then Laurence would distribute the wealth and cast off his false identity. He would use his share of the funds to reclaim their lands, the way their father had always intended.

And she would—

Kahldar shifted against her body.

Selida froze.

She saw him waking in the empty, quiet bedroll. Watched faith turn to disbelief. It would not take him long to find the treasure room, empty. His expression—the heart she'd told him she would guard—would break.

She saw him across from her, then, amid a row of Dawnland knights, all in full plate, banners waving. His helm would be down, but there would be no mistaking the way he sat, easy and graceful, on Ispen's black back.

Selida closed her eyes as despair reached into her, cold fingers hungry.

She had waited too long. Three days ago, even, this

plan might have worked. But after last night's bloodshed —even if Laurence had the funds, he could never reclaim their properties now. Hundreds of his own men had seen him spill the blood of his Dawnland neighbors.

No, if she gave him the treasure, he would raise a full rebellion of coastal lords, backed by the Church. And, so committed, they would fight, all or nothing, to return their home to the place of wealth and freedom they remembered.

That is what you want, is it not?

It didn't matter that all her attempts to come to parlay had failed. It didn't matter that she had prolonged this stalemate for weeks, looking for a peaceful solution. It didn't matter that dozens of souls had passed into Aluna's keeping on account of her floundering.

This moment would change the fate of the Tidelands. It was her very last chance to salvage something worth saving from this horrific disaster.

If you do not act, you will regret this for the rest of your life.

It should be the easiest thing in the world to part herself from this bed, from the side of this sanctimonious Welded Dawnlander, and finish the work she had come here to do.

But Kahldar's breath was even on her skin, and his steady exhalations held her fixed in place. She wondered if their bodies had sealed together where they joined.

The minutes crawled over her. Even inaction was a choice. Dawn crept nearer; her perfect window was clos-ing. She heard Emmeline's voice in her mind: *It is not only the days you expect to change your life which have the power to do so.*

Unbidden, her hand curled into his.

I love him.

I promised I would not betray him.

She turned her head into the pillow so her tears would not wake him.

Tidemother, what do You need me to do?

The pearl had held no answers. Stirred by her involuntary shudders, Kahldar murmured in his sleep, and pulled her closer. She soothed his matted hair back from his forehead.

You claimed my vow, and myself, for Aluna, he had said.

Her breath stilled.

Have I... read You wrong?

All at once the empty chair transformed from a disappointment into a promise.

She imagined the divine voice so clearly: *It is your choice, beloved daughter.*

And wasn't that why she loved Aluna? The Tidemother granted her the independence to choose. If *this* was the decision her heart demanded, was there some chance it was the right one, and not just an abject betrayal?

Perhaps, Selida thought, she had already made up her mind, many times over: once at the joust, when he had offered her the victor's crown, then on the wall, when she had saved his life, and yet again last night, when she had banished his fears and taken his trust.

Maybe the window was not closing. Maybe it had closed a long time ago, with her none the wiser.

The passing minutes teased her with visions of everything she was about to surrender.

Enough.

She had decided.

After weeks of sleepless dithering, it was simple: Here was the right choice, at last. If it was a betrayal of decades of her own resentment, then so be it. Now, her task was to do *something* to make sure she didn't destroy everyone who trusted her.

Selida closed her eyes, leaned her forehead against the crown of Kahldar's head, and began to plot anew.

K ahldar woke in the watery light before dawn. His mind was at peace, and his body content. No trace of emptiness or uncertainty lingered—at last, he and his intent were one. *Selida loves me.* It was impossible, and yet, he believed her. A world of grim responsibilities lay just beyond her blue chapel door, but he could hold them at bay by lingering a lifetime in this moment.

The scent of her infused the pillow and covers. Her skin, alas, no longer pressed warm against him.

Reluctantly, he opened his eyes.

Sometime in the night, Selida had drawn the feather coverlet up around them. She lay in its warm cocoon, close but not touching. She'd been watching him for some time, he guessed: eyes steady, brow creased, lips set in an earnest line.

A coldness stole back into his chest. He frowned, and reached up to trace her cheek. "I am sorry. Was this not what you sought?"

She closed her eyes, caught his hand in hers, and turned her head to kiss his palm. "It was... far more than what I had intended."

Ah. "More is not always better."

"I suppose you'd know."

"Yes."

She opened her eyes, and took a deep breath. "Kahldar, what would you say if I told you that I knew a way to end the siege, today? Make sure that not one more man dies?"

His skin chilled as she invited the rest of the world back into their sanctuary. He drew a breath. "Do you truly believe a peaceful resolution is still possible?" He imagined what would happen when the King's taxmen came over the hill, in three or more weeks' time. The Fox commanded far more men than they'd first estimated. Would Wyvernsvow still fly young Lydris's pennants? Or would the Fox sit in the great hall, surrounded by treasure and turncoats? Either way, at least one bloodbath loomed before them.

Her lips were as grave as he had ever seen them. "Kahldar, it is not only possible, but now essential. If we let the current state of affairs run its course, there will be so much violence that war will rage for a generation. Maybe more."

He nodded soberly, tracing her ear with his fingertip. "What do you propose?"

Her eyes burned into him as she spoke. "First you must know this: The Fox of the Tidelands is my brother, Laurence Coralglass."

TWENTY-TWO

Kahldar stopped breathing.

Selida continued: "If you and I wed, today, Laurence would risk excommunication if he continued the siege."

Kahldar could barely hear her. Her voice dissolved into noise as blood roared in his ears. Finally he choked out, "Pardon?"

"You are Wyvernsvow's commander. I heard you swear those oaths to Lady Magnus and young Lord Lydris yesterday. If we publish our banns and invite Laurence to the ceremony, he would have no choice but to order his men to retreat."

Kahldar's mouth, working faster than his heart, managed, "The Fox's men are pirates and bandits. Would they accept this reversal?"

"His trusted commanders are knights, just like you. And all of them know the King's taxmen are coming. They would adhere to an honorable call to retreat if we appeased their pride."

He opened his mouth to object, but she plowed on. "So, in addition to our marriage, we must give them *one* item from the treasury: Aluna's pearl."

"Selida—"

"It would not just be an appeasement. We would offer it to my brother as your Dawnlander bride gift. And, by Tidelander tradition, Laurence too would owe me a bride gift. Instead of funds, I will accept a cessation of hostilities, now and forevermore." She scoured his expression. "That should satisfy both his pride and that of the men who follow him."

Kahldar lay perfectly still and forced himself to count his heartbeats.

When he was eight, his uncle had taken him fishing. It was the dead of winter, and he had chased one of their dogs too far out over the ice. He heard the same cracking sound now, felt the same moment of vertigo before the murderous cold entombed him.

"But... what if he's changed?" he said. "Even if he was once the brother you grew up with, how can you know the Fox will now react as you hope? And that his men would be willing to cooperate?"

"Ah." Her expression drained of color, her fingers of warmth.

It came out harder than he intended: "Tell me."

She inhaled. "I know because I came to Wyvernsvow to betray the castle."

The water closed over his head. It was every bit as terrible as he remembered. Unthinking, he sat up. *"Selida."*

She rose with him. The cover fell to her waist, but he dared not look away from her ashen face. Her fingers, still caught in his, squeezed. "I am sorry."

His thoughts slowed. He forced himself to remember her on the parapet, dragging the wounded back from the front lines. He saw her in the caverns, stone flowing and splitting into serpents. He saw her at the cistern, clean water rising as she prayed.

He closed his eyes for what felt like a very long time. When at last he opened them, he asked simply: "Selida, if you came to betray the castle, why does it yet stand?"

"What?"

"You have said it yourself. If you had wanted the castle to fall, you could have poisoned the men, sickened the young lord, or left us to the Fox's mercy on the parapet."

"I..." Her voice trailed off.

"Exoeras, if you had wished to undermine the foundation and drop the keep straight into the sea, I am certain you would have found a way."

She flushed. "I failed, alright?" She shifted, but he refused to release her hands. "I couldn't bring myself to fulfill the Grand Cleric's orders. Day after day, I weighed my options. Every time, I decided that I would risk no harm to Aluna's faithful as long as there was a chance that I could accomplish my ends bloodlessly."

The pieces were beginning to fall together, but he dared not stop until he truly understood, lest an even greater misunderstanding hide within her words. "Your Grand Cleric knew of this? She charged you to aid the Fox? Has she not sworn fealty to King Harald?"

"Yes, but—"

"But?"

"But, as a Tidelander, she could not let him reduce Aluna's ancient treasures to mere gold and gems for his coffers. So when..."

"When what?"

The words came out in a rush, like she knew she ought not to be saying them. "So when Laurence came to her, looking for a way to liberate the treasure and buy our family's lands out of debt, she pledged the Church's support to the Fox and ordered me to find some way to ease his passage."

"She knew you've served this castle faithfully for years." Anger, again—not at Selida, but on her behalf. "How could she order you to do this?"

She looked at first baffled, and then stung. "Because she valued my capabilities?"

"Why did you not tell her it was dishonorable?"

"I... that is not the coin we trade."

He shook his head. "Even if you could not dissuade her from this plan, why commit yourself to it? Surely she has other clerics."

Bemusement crept into her chagrin. "The... past decades have been unkind to the devotees of Aluna.

Another cleric sent in my place might have less incentive to keep it simple."

Kahldar laced his fingers deeper into her trembling ones. "So... you meant to do this... this *thing* peacefully."

"I did." She swallowed. "Obviously, I failed."

"Why did you think that a bloodless..."—he did not want to say the words *coup* or *treason*, did not even want to think them—"...that it would be possible to avoid bloodshed?"

Her fingers tightened in his. "Emmeline and I were friends, once. Her husband was a reasonable man, and I knew you and even Ser Aegison had some measure of concern for the people of the coast."

"And so you tried to persuade us to parlay."

"Well, first I tried to convince Emmeline to declare herself sole ruler of Wyvernsvow. If she held it as a Skyfawn, rather than as a regent for her son, the dispossessed coastal knights would have sworn their fealty. Think of that: a coronation, in lieu of a siege."

He blinked, appalled. *A coronation, followed by a very different siege.* Keeping his voice carefully neutral, he said merely, "The King would consider that rebellion."

She straightened, the ghost of an old indignation rising. "Emmeline Skyfawn and Lydris Magnus wed to stop the war. Both families used their power to quell dissent—on both sides. Why should all the loyalty due her legacy become subsumed into his? Life on the coast is perilous. What if she or her son perishes? Should not her blood kin have some stake in continuing the peace? And if the Fox and his displaced Tidelanders saw one of their own rise in your King's service, they too might commit to a joint path forward."

He opened his mouth to list the thousand reasons such logic would bear no weight in the Dawnlands; thankfully, she cut him off.

"Anyway, it did not matter because Emmeline did not want to follow that road."

"Thank Exoeras," he breathed.

She glowered at him. "*Then* I attempted to parlay. You agreed that my logic about the treasury was reasonable."

"I did. And I mentioned it to Ser Aegison, that morning. He, alas, did not agree. I am sorry I did not have an opportunity to tell you this before you approached him on the matter."

Her lips twitched. "And I am sorry I thought you craven in your silence."

The events of the siege continued to tumble through his mind. "In the dungeon. Did you provoke Ser Aegison on purpose?"

She made a face. "No. I—hadn't had much sleep the night before. I could not stomach his utter disregard for the Church's Law of Salvage. I lost my temper."

"That is what I suspected. And was the prisoner telling the truth, when he said he went to your lantern? Did you, in fact, walk the parapets to show the Fox where to attack?"

"Emmeline was the one who ordered me to bring you tea."

He held her gaze, waiting.

"Very well, I thought to use the opportunity to show the Fox that the walls were too fortified to attack."

"But he found a gap in the rotation."

She shrugged. "I didn't think it was large enough. And I still don't know why they fought with naked blades."

"That is common, in war." Now it was his turn to sound bemused.

"Yes, but the Grand Cleric implied to me that Laurence wanted a peaceful resolution. He hopes one day to reclaim our father's lands. Perhaps his own men had different ideas."

"And the sappers?"

"Was them taking their own initiative." She sighed. "Perhaps they tired of waiting for my message."

"What message?"

"That I had opened the postern gate." Her eyes were black. "If parlay did not work, the Grand Cleric and I judged that the simplest solution."

He disappeared into the water again. The ice closed over his head. Kahldar felt like her grip on his hands was the only thing anchoring him to the present.

"Thank you," he managed at last, "for not opening the postern gate during the sortie. I do not think it would have ended well for Lord Lydris and his mother if the Fox had entered the keep while its commander was away."

He watched her eyebrows melt upwards. "What? No. Even with your force absent, the keep was still full of men, ready and awake."

"All the same. I thank you."

Her smile was humorless. "Kahldar, if I had wanted to let the Fox through the gate at a time when the keep was truly exhausted and disorganized, then I should have done so three hours ago."

He digested this.

It wasn't a lake in winter, and he wasn't drowning. He was here, in her chapel. Through the slats in the shutters, he could see shafts of Exos's light poking holes through the clouds to caress the surface of the sea.

At last he said: "But you are here."

"I am here," she echoed.

He looked down at their twined hands and wondered again about bodies and souls. What was merged could yet be sundered. "Thank you for telling me this."

She let him gather his thoughts for three whole minutes. Then: "Before you hang me for treason, I would like to know the answer to my question."

"Which question?"

"Kahldar. Will you marry me?"

He gave her his sternest look. "I do not know."

Her mouth opened.

"I need to think."

He heard her jaw click shut. "Well enough. But don't think too long."

"I will give you my answer anon." He rose, and drew her up beside him. "Until then, will you dress and accompany me on my rounds?"

A ghost of her smile touched her eyes. "Don't Dawnlanders sometimes parade their prisoners around naked before an execution? Is your exhortation to dress a sign of clemency?"

"If you do not bait me, I promise you a better chance at an affirmative answer."

Completely naked, she dipped him a meek little curtsey, undercut by the editorial pucker of her lips. Then she handed him his smallclothes.

The storm had rinsed the black from the horizon. For the first time in weeks, Kahldar could see blue streaks of sky through clouds rushed overhead by a stiff autumnal breeze. As he walked the parapet, counting men and receiving assurances that the Fox's army had not moved from its camp, his mind began to settle. He had worried that Selida's presence would feel like a live coal, burning in the back of his brain, but instead she felt familiar, as though they had walked this way together for not merely weeks, but years.

When they descended into the bailey, the two little girls from the road approached to ask for blessings. Selida's transparent patience, he thought, was not so much a mask drawn over a fevered heart as a devout fulfillment of her duty: to embody her Goddess for Her worshippers.

No wonder he had suspected nothing.

They entered the great hall, and Selida paused at the side of a page who had lost fingers to the grappling ladders. Eight souls had passed in the night, a chambermaid told them. Selida stopped by knots of the bereaved and sang them quiet prayers.

In the kitchens, they accepted a breakfast of fresh bread and thin sliced cheese. They ate in silence, standing at the doorway that looked out over the practice yard. Pages ran pieces of dented armor and weapons to the blacksmith, whose forge shimmered heat into the morning air.

"Shall we visit the stables?" Selida asked. The wind swirled her dark blue skirts over his boots.

He found he did not need to. "Let us return to the chapel."

K ahldar closed the door behind them. Selida's expression was still bland, but she sat down before the banked fire, clasped her hands, and then immediately rose again to open the shutters. Aluna's sea was almost blue.

He went to her. She held out a hand, and he took it.

"Selida," he said, "I cannot say that your confession sits easy with me, but I do know this: You are still the woman I believed you to be. Despite your orders, you remained loyal to the people of this keep."

Her eyes were unreadable. "But?"

"But it was made quite clear to me that you would rather die of starvation than bind yourself to a Dawnlander." Concern creased his brow. "Is averting war today worth all your many tomorrows?"

A rueful breath escaped her lips. "Kahldar, I realized early this morning that you have come to be first in my heart: over my family, over my people, over my long resentment. Perhaps even over Aluna, though I hope it never comes to that." She shrugged through his sharp inhalation and continued: "What are the relative strictures of marriage compared to this? Was I so blind to what you have become to me that my Goddess had to make the fate of the Tidelands contingent on our joining before I could see?"

"I... oh." Relief, awe, and gratitude warred with alarm in his breast. Cautiously, he asked, "Is putting a man before your Goddess not... blasphemy?"

Her smile slid sideways. "Your Welded assumptions about religion never cease to amaze me. If it were blasphemy, then why did She make you so beautiful? Your eyes so keen and your heart so open? Why do I feel your integrity as a tangible force on my skin?"

He stopped breathing.

It was her turn to look down at their entwined hands. "And you? Until last night, I thought you would never risk your heart outside the confines of wedlock."

He waited until her aqua eyes were again fixed on his face. "Last night, you promised to allay my fears. Even against the demands of kin and of Church, you upheld that promise. Now you offer to extend that vow, into perpetuity, at great personal cost."

Her mouth trembled. "It's true I do not always trust your Dawnlander customs. But I do trust *you*, Kahldar.

Were we to wed, I do not know what shape the rest of our days would take, but I know I will find the answer more palatable than the alternative. I do not want a life without you."

Kahldar looked down into her luminous expression. "Selida, you have captivated me from the moment I first saw you. I suspected that I loved you for some time; watching you champion and minister to your people with such fierce, unbridled determination, I knew it for certain. It seemed impossible to express that love honorably, as it deserved—as you deserved—but here we stand, both changed. I was honored to spend last night by your side, and it would be the greatest honor of my life to discover who we will become, pledged each to the other forevermore."

Then he pulled her close, and held her so tight that she gasped.

Her voice was muffled. "Do you still worry I will sunder your soul?"

"No, beloved. For it belongs to you now, and I know how jealously you guard that which is yours."

She wrapped her arms with equal strength around him, and neither of them moved for a very long time.

TWENTY-THREE

Selida found Lydris and his mother in the great hall. Emmeline knelt at a wounded yeoman's side, wrapping his bloodied shoulder. She wore her sleeves tied back, and a cooking apron protected her plain kirtle. Blood flecked her arms to the elbow. Lydris stood nearby, dutifully holding a roll of bandages.

Emmeline looked up from her work. Her golden hair glinted in the morning light, the only clean thing in the room. "A blessed sight you are, Lady Cleric. I'm sure many of these people would prefer your even hand to my unpracticed one."

The man she was helping shook his head as vigorously as his injuries would allow. "Nay! Bless you, milady. For your defense of us last night, and for your tending now."

Emmeline hushed him, and Selida bowed her head. "I

will lead prayers for the wounded soon. But first, may I request a private moment?"

Emmeline took in Selida and Kahldar, who stood silently behind her. Her eyes narrowed. "Let us adjourn to the solar. My apartments are serving as sickrooms for the moment." She handed her apron to a village lady and washed her hands in the basin. Lydris left the bandages in a neat pile on a table.

Once in the quiet room, Selida told Emmeline everything. "In conclusion," she finished, "I request from you Ser Kahldar's hand in marriage. As regent of his liege, Lord Lydris, will you give us your blessing? If you are willing to perform the ceremony, I can invest you with the authority to act as our officiant."

Emmeline sat back in her chair, eyes round with equal parts horror and an even more horrifying delight. "How astonishing." Then she looked at Kahldar, standing just beside the door. His face wore its customary wooden expression. "Pray tell, do you approve of this marriage, Ser Kahldar?"

His reply was certain and sure. "Yes, my lady. I do."

Emmeline turned back to Selida, who felt very alone in the center of the solar. "Will he dance the tide ceremonies with you?" Her eyes grew even rounder. "Or does he plan to take orders, so you may marry and practice in the Welded fashion?"

The Grand Cleric would have a fit. "If we resolve the siege today, I expect we will have a lifetime to address such quandaries."

Emmeline pursed her lips. "And what of his family? They are landed, are they not? What if their tangled succession calls him home to the Dawnlands?"

At this, Lord Lydris burst in: "But Ser Kahldar, your home is here."

Kahldar bowed. "Aye, my lord." A smile touched his lips as he regarded the other three. "It is."

"At the very least, you would be expected to travel with Selida as she does her rounds on the coast," Emmeline said. "Unless you plan to petition the Grand Cleric to take a permanent position here at Wyvernsvow?" Her gaze moved back to Selida. "You *are* a trifle advanced in years to be gallivanting from community to community."

In a moment, Selida knew, Emmeline would jump to the topic of future offspring. "As I said," she interrupted, "once the question of marriage is settled, we will have ample time to answer these other questions."

"You seem in great haste."

"I would like to send the banns to my brother before he renews his attack on the keep."

"And what would persuade Lord Coralglass to attend this happy event? Given your long estrangement?"

"That's what Aluna's pearl will accomplish, I hope."

Emmeline drummed her fingers on the arm of her chair. Finally, she mused, "I cannot help but notice similarities to the very plan you had at the outset of the siege. The one which I bade you surrender. Multiple times."

"And I have bowed to your wisdom as requested," Selida said. "Multiple times."

"And yet here we are."

"The situation has changed, and the plan been much improved by your influence. Was it not you who ordered me to take tea to the battlements?"

Lydris, following this exchange like he would the volley of a shuttlecock, lost his patience. He bounced twice in his chair. "Mother, is this not the sort of question you would usually defer to Ser Aegison? Is that not Ser Kahldar's responsibility now?" He turned to his practice yard hero. "What do you think, Ser Kahldar? Is this a chivalrous plan?"

Selida watched Kahldar step forward, dropping his mask of blank neutrality. Walking halfway into the room, he knelt respectfully in Lydris's direction.

"I appreciate your trust, my liege. However, now that Ser Aegison has fallen in the fulfillment of his duties, control of your regency reverts to your mother. I submit myself to her judgment, in proxy of yours."

Emmeline considered him. "Is this not an authority you would like to assume? King Harald is not present to grant it to you, but I am sure he would understand and approve if you were to take it up."

Kahldar glanced at Selida.

Say your heart.

He remained silent for a long moment before speaking. "I believe King Harald acted with wisdom when he entrusted Ser Aegison with primary responsibility for your regency," he told Lydris. "Your mother was freshly burdened by grief, and the position forged Garret's loyalty into an unbreakable bulwark for her and for yourself. However, owing to his lack of firsthand experience in the Tidelands, I also believe His Majesty may have underestimated the capabilities of its daughters." He sent another glance Selida's way before turning back to young Lydris. "Your regency is now properly returned to your mother, and my oaths demand I support her vision for the future of your lands. This gladdens me, for no soul alive better understands your two heritages. I trust her to build a peaceful future for all who dwell in your domain."

Emmeline blinked. "You have an unexpected gift with words." Even Lydris looked thoughtful.

"Thank you, my lady; perhaps. But I pray it will remain untested," Kahldar said.

"You are content to serve me in this capacity?"

"I am."

"As Ser Aegison did?"

"As faithfully, yes. Though my interpretation of the King's justice is less traditional than his was, as you are aware."

Emmeline nodded. "Thank you, Ser Kahldar. Your counsel will bring a welcome steadiness to the region, once peace is again within our grasp."

Lydris turned to his mother. "Does that mean you get to decide whether Ser Kahldar can marry Lady Selida?"

She smiled at him. "So it would seem. But, before I decide: What do you think, my love? What would you have me do, for your people?"

Lydris considered the question carefully. "We didn't

accept the parlay because Ser Aegison said the Fox could not really hurt the people in the keep. He also said the King's taxmen would arrive before we starved." He glanced at Selida. "I wrote that letter to our allies to hurry their reinforcements."

Selida curtseyed.

"But it turns out that even if the taxmen do arrive soon, the Fox can indeed reach us, and hurt the people." His gaze turned inward. Selida could see him recalling the long night in the caves, and the rows of wounded in the great hall. "If we can prevent more pain and death, then parlay is the right thing to do," Lydris said to his mother. Then, quickly: "Or is it weak of me to think that?"

"Friendship and peace are never weak, so long as you believe they will be met in kind," Lady Magnus said with a smile. "Thank you for your counsel. Why don't you and Ser Kahldar step into the hallway? This was Lady Selida's plan, and she and I must consult in private before I commit to it."

Kahldar glanced at her. Selida nodded.

"As you will, milady." He held out his hand for Lord Lydris, who gave them both another glance before allowing himself to be led into the corridor. "We will be outside."

The door closed behind them.

Selida rose out of her curtsey. "With all due respect, Emmeline, you are having too much fun with this."

"We must all find our entertainment where we can."

Selida, to her immense chagrin, found herself blushing.

Standing, Emmeline came to take Selida's hands in her own. The older woman's fingers were warm, for once. "Selida. The King's men will come. The castle can endure a little longer. Are you really willing to go through with this? To give up a singular existence, dedicated to yourself and to the Tidelands, for the love of a man and a marriage to bind our peoples together?"

"I am." Then she sighed. "I expect all this compromise will be a great deal of bother, but I trust we will find our way forward. It is the least we can do for the generation that follows us. Better to leave them an imperfect peace than a legacy of blood and vengeance."

"You won't be able to take this back. Do you truly believe this, heart and body? Do you pledge to commit the rest of your days to this project?"

"I do." She was silent for a long moment. "Though I have never felt so naked."

"Action in the face of vulnerability is the stuff of courage." Emmeline looked down. "And I suppose if you've found your courage in this, the least I can do is my part regarding Lydris's regency." She inhaled. "You were right that I let myself trust Ser Aegison blindly, relying on him like a babe upon her parent. It was ill done of me. In the future, I will expect my lieutenants to respect my counsel in exchange for their authority."

"The people and your neighboring lords will be grateful," Selida said. "I thank you on their behalf."

"You need not look so grim," Emmeline said.

Selida was silent. Eventually she managed, "This is the annihilation of everything I was."

"Mmm. Ser Kahldar, too, moves with the air of a changed man."

"We are both new-made this morning."

"Oh, I would not go that far. Violently rearranged, perhaps."

"Perhaps."

The lines at the corners of Emmeline's eyes deepened. "You do know this will mean adhering to his standards of wedded chastity, do you not?"

"I do."

"Are you not finding at least some speck of joy in all of this?"

"Some speck." Selida felt her mouth turn up at the corner. "Despite all my better sense."

"On the contrary, it seems to me like you have at last stopped fighting a war that ended a score of years ago. That is very good sense."

"You may say 'I told you so.'"

"As a good liege, I would—and should—never."

Selida took a deep breath. "There's something else I need to ask of you."

"Goodness. How grave you look. Yes?"

"Can you teach me how to make a wreath? Of wheat? I think it needs to be braided."

Emmeline burst out laughing. "Of *winter* wheat?"

Selida reddened further. "Yes."

Emmeline leaned away from her, eyes twinkling. "It is the wrong time of year for winter wheat."

"Normal wheat, then. Straw, even."

Emmeline squeezed Selida's hands. "To make it a proper gift to a prospective Dawnlander husband, you will have to braid the wreath yourself. But I would be happy to walk you through the fundamentals. You will do quite well at this, I promise."

CHAPTER

TWENTY-FOUR

They held the wedding, such as it was, on the parapet overlooking the road. After weeks of muddy weather, the crisp ocean wind had scoured the noon sky into a dome of livid cerulean. Cheers sounded throughout the morning as guardsmen watched the Fox's boats disappear in ones and twos like dust swept over the horizon.

Wyvernsvow's banners streamed perpendicular to their posts, and the brisk gusts clawed Selida's hair out of its loops. She trusted that even if their vows bounced erratically past the crowd, so too would any errant arrows from below. All the same, Kahldar had insisted she wear her breastplate over her festival robes.

He stood across from her now, still clad in Ser Aegison's cuirass, though Lord Magnus's teal and gold tabard hid it from view. Amidst the spate of letters exchanged between Wyvernsvow and the Fox's camp the previous day, there had been no time for Kahldar to properly polish his armor. Even so, the brilliant sunlight now struck it with such force that Selida knew she would remember it to be shining: as bright as his eyes had been that morning when she had given him the little braided wreath.

"I'm afraid it's not winter wheat. Ah... it's straw, actually. And Emmeline had to help me with braiding it."

Kahldar's callused fingers had cradled the lopsided circlet as though it were made of gold. "It is perfect." His smiling eyes rose to meet hers. "A reminder of my past, and a symbol of our future. I will treasure it always."

"Shall we begin?" Emmeline asked. The Lady of Wyvernsvow had retired her black robes, shocking the assembled farmers, fishermen, and guardsmen. Today her kirtle and hennin matched the clear fall sky, and her veil was white—the colors of the Tidelander royal family. Lydris, beside her, carried a basket fashioned of seagrass. Inside sat a silk and velvet bundle.

Emmeline took Selida's right hand, and Kahldar's left. Smiling for the crowds draping the parapet, the stairs, and the bailey, she also turned her head to acknowledge the trio of knights just visible on a rise beyond Wyvernsvow's walls. They stood, mounted and helmed, comfortably out of arrow-flight. Emmeline pitched her voice to cut through the wind.

"We gather today to witness how the serpents of the sky have bound this man, Ser Kahldar Whitepeak, and this woman, Lady Selida Coralglass, in mutual affection and trust."

It was so strange, Selida thought, to hear the words in a voice not her own. Across the little space, she caught Kahldar's gaze. At his steady calm, the trembles in her body subsided. She wondered if his smile would ever not leave her breathless. The next thing she knew, the ceremony was drawing to a close.

"—and by the power vested in me by Aluna, Tide-mother and Goddess of the Moon and All Serpents, I now pronounce you husband and wife. May your union be writ plain for all your fellows to see, until the ocean consumes every last mountain upon the earth." Then Emmeline raised their hands, and joined them together.

Two of Kahldar's knights lifted their bugles and blared a single, bright note. Their testimonial to the exchange of vows echoed over the peninsula, reaching whatever ears Emmeline's words had not.

Old Meg stepped forward then, to lay an embroidered cloth on the floor at their feet. Lydris's nurse had brought it by Selida's chapel that morning for a blessing.

"Well, you certainly found a way forward," she had said.

Selida had smiled. "Shall I give Laurence your greetings?"

"Do not bother. I am done with such things. Tell that to your meddling aunt, too."

Selida had looked out the window, at the blue sea. "This is the better way."

"It is so because you choose it," the nurse had intoned.

Now, Old Meg placed Selida's silver bowl on the blessed cloth. Emmeline accepted an ewer from Dame Pottage and poured a measure of seawater over Selida and Kahldar's clasped hands. The liquid caught the light and swirled into the bowl like a stream of incandescent serpents.

Selida tightened her fingers around Kahldar's and gathered her split skirts. Together, they stepped over the silver moon. Their reflections crossed that of the open sky.

"Ser Kahldar, you may now kiss our lady cleric," Emmeline said.

Kahldar lifted Selida's hands to his lips, and bowed deeply. The people of the keep cheered, the roar growing and surrounding them like the sound of the tide in the caverns.

"Is something amiss?" Selida murmured. "It is common for the bridal kiss to be on the lips."

Kahldar's cheeks colored. "In... public?" Wrapping her in his arms instead, he told her, "I must confess I find the thought of my homeland being swallowed by the sea somewhat more alarming than romantic."

"On the contrary," Selida said, "as your stalwart peaks will never wear away, they protect our bond by their mere stubborn existence."

He smiled at this, and Selida used the opportunity to pull his mouth down to hers. The cheering grew louder, punctuated by answering bugles from the three knights on the road.

Selida released Kahldar's neck, but did not step out of the circle of his arms.

Lydris approached, basket proffered, eyes serious. "Is it time?"

Selida looked out at the distant rise, and the man bearing the faceless armor and black shield. "It is," she said.

The young lord held on to the basket for a moment longer, as if part of him yearned to pull the pearl from its velvet sack and sink back into its visions.

"You never showed me Aluna's snakes," he had pouted yesterday, when she had returned his coin.

"Then come with me to the caves and watch," Selida had said.

When they were again crouched over the black trove, she dipped a finger into the water. Coldfire eels flooded towards her out of the shadows. At her bidding, they nosed through the treasure until they found Aluna's pale orb. Floating it on their backs, they swam in increasingly tight circles until she and Lydris could no longer see the glint of gold between their forms. Selida bid him lift the knot of them, now a contoured seagrass basket, out of the water.

"You could have gotten the pearl yourself any time!" the boy had exclaimed as he turned the basket over and over in his hands.

"You're right," Selida had said, looking at Kahldar. "But it would not have been worth the price."

Now, Lydris gave the basket to her still-blushing

groom. "As your liege, I present you with a bride gift worthy of Lady Selida," he recited loudly. "Please offer it to her family on our behalf."

Composing himself, Kahldar knelt and bowed his head. "I pray they will find it acceptable, though even so precious a relic cannot compare to her priceless worth. Thank you for your generosity and wisdom, my lord. You've returned tenfold the trust I placed in you. May you rule long and well. May the Dominion endure, embracing Dawnlands and Tidelands alike. And may Wyvernsvow ever stand, proud vanguard of a better future."

Lydris frowned as the crowd erupted in another round of deafening cheers. "We won't let anything happen to you, Ser Kahldar. Our archers are watching for any sign of treachery."

"Even still," Emmeline broke in, pulling her son close, "the things we want most must sometimes be spoken into the breeze, if only so that Her serpents may carry them to Her ears. How else is She to ensure that our fondest prayers become the foundation of all our tomorrows?"

The newlyweds stood on the road, the drawbridge closed behind them. Knocked arrows bristled over the walls, making Selida's skin itch. She wondered how many answering archers the Fox had hidden in the nearby scrub. Kahldar, she felt, was far too exposed, despite the protective prayers she had woven around them both.

At another blast of trumpetry, the three knights cantered down the path towards them. The one on the left Selida did not recognize, but the one on the right was a head and a half taller than most men. An unhappily familiar mace hung over his shoulder, light leaking out from between its wrappings. And the knight in the middle...

Her brother too wore plate, and a black band on his arm to honor the men he had lost. When he was a good twenty feet away, he raised a fist. His outriders stopped, and he removed his helmet. Beside her, Kahldar grimaced. She probably should have warned him that she and her sibling were famously alike in features.

"I got your invitation, Selida," Laurence said, as if a decade had not passed since she'd seen him last. "It was beautifully written, and delivered into my hand by a particularly venomous species of asp." He smiled his charming smile, and his sand-colored ringlets seemed to move of their own accord in the cheerful sunlight. "Have you really gone and wed a Dawnlander? Father would have been so... vindicated."

"I stopped doing things just to infuriate him when he died," Selida answered. "Thank you for coming." She held out the basket, its velvets pulled back to reveal Aluna's pearl. It still glowed with its own light, and she could feel its whispers caressing the skin of her fingers.

"You know," Laurence said, "outing me like this is going to make it very hard to reclaim our lands by legal means."

Selida choked as words piled up in her throat. Kahldar squeezed her hand. It helped. She managed a lopsided smile. "Perhaps you will consult me directly the next time you decide to besiege a castle on my holy circuit."

"We've certainly left a snarl in your Grand Cleric's tapestry. Do you think Auntie will forgive us?"

"As much as I love her," Selida said, "I must act as Aluna bids me."

Laurence touched his hand respectfully to his forelock, and then turned to Kahldar. "Before I dismount, I should ask if this is an ambush. Are you waiting to avenge your fallen commander?"

"It is not an ambush," Kahldar replied.

Laurence's grin didn't fade as he hopped off his horse. "I'm going to love being your brother," he said.

"Ser Kahldar can join the list of people who would like to throttle you, but are forbidden by Aluna from doing so."

"Does he tolerate queues? The list has grown since we last spoke."

Selida passed the basket to Kahldar, who stepped forward to present it to Laurence. "I offer this on behalf of my liege and family, in exchange for your sister's hand in marriage," Kahldar pronounced, expressionless.

Taking the gift, Laurence replied, "And I accept on behalf of my family, though I really ought to remind you that it has been illegal to buy or sell people for the last hundred years. Here on the civilized coast, anyway."

"*Laurence,*" Selida warned.

He nodded briskly. "Right; and, as my bride gift to my sister, I formally offer to take my people and depart your lands." He turned back to Selida. "May you bring these riches with you into your new family, and thereby secure your standing in your new house."

"By Aluna's blessing, so be it," Selida said.

Laurence turned the basket over in his hands. "Tide-mother, are these coldfire eels?"

"They'll return to life if you leave them in seawater for a day," Selida said. "Handle them with care, please." Then she picked up a second basket she had brought out of the castle with her. "Lady Magnus's message suggested a wedding feast. I brought enough scones for you and your men, should you wish to partake."

Laurence bowed. "Your scones? I could not refuse, but I will take mine to go."

His face sobered. For a moment, as the weight of recent years fell over his features, it was as if their father lived again; their little broken family reunited at last. What he would have said about all of this, Selida dared not imagine.

Laurence had no such compunctions. He tilted his head back to take in all of Wyvernsvow's lopsided bulk. "I suppose it's not falling into the sea anytime soon after all."

Kahldar twitched.

"We'll just have to end the war in some other way," Selida said. "Refraining from renewing it seems like a good start."

Her little brother smiled. Simple as that, Selida felt their father's ghost dissolve like mist over the ocean. She could have hugged Laurence. But he stepped back, his expression light, and bowed. "I expect to see you again soon, dear sister."

Scone between his teeth and eelweave basket in one hand, the Fox jumped back on his horse and galloped his men away.

Selida and Kahldar watched the trio ride up the path, past the scrub. Then they watched the bushes rustle, as the men hidden therein retreated back up the hill.

Kahldar squinted after them. "I begin to understand how he has been such a wily opponent, and so beloved of his people and Goddess alike. Even parted by a chasm of time, you share an aspect."

Denial bubbled up in her throat, but none of it stood up to scrutiny. Instead she shrugged. "You are family, now."

"Which shall make the coming years exceedingly... interesting, I am sure."

"At least we shall never grow into one of those couples who sits in silence before the fire, words exhausted." Gently, she let herself lean against his side. His immovable warmth soothed away the prickles of unease she felt, imagining all the things that were yet to come.

"I will not worry," he said, "so long as you promise to always tell me what is on your mind, and in your heart."

"Only if you promise to help me solve my problems, instead of critiquing how I came by them."

He touched his chest. "I promise."

Behind them, Selida heard the guards start to lower the drawbridge. A babble of blessed normalcy leaked out from the courtyard: fishermen eager to refill the larders, farmers excited to salvage whatever remained of the harvest. Children and pigs, horses and cows: a normal autumn day at Wyvernsvow.

Beside her, Selida felt Kahldar relax at last. She lifted the basket of scones. "Before we return, would you like a blandishment? I made them with citrus and the last of the honey."

Instead of answering, he squared her against him and kissed her—first chastely, and then not. When he finally drew away, she was still assessing the impact on her extremities as he reached into the basket. "Thank you," he said. "Though I wish they were called something else."

She steadied her breath. "If you like, I can make scones for everyone else. But blandishments only for you."

He bit into the pastry, and she saw him close his eyes to appreciate the sting of citrus and savor the aroma of butter. "I will treasure them," he said. "As I will all your many gifts, all the days of our lives."

And together, they walked back into the keep.

APPENDIX A: HISTORY
TIMELINE OF THE DAWNLANDER INVASION

Compiled for Grand Cleric Jadea Coralglass by Quillkeeper Penrose of the Church of Aluna in the summer of 1135

1080 – King Carlon of the Dawnland Dominion approaches Prince Everett Skyfawn to negotiate access to our coastal ports. The Church of Aluna cautions the Prince against this, as the Dawnland Dominion is a recent convert to the Welded "religion" of the south, and many kingdoms so infected by this "faith" exhibit evangelist and expansionist behavior. Seeking fresh profit, Prince Skyfawn conducts talks with the Dominion anyway. The Treaty of the Ports is written.

1085 – Incompetent at sea, King Carlon's advisors claim their goods are becoming lost on the coast and demand to send more troops to protect their shipments from "pirates." When their efforts prove unsuccessful, Dawnland "knights" resort to taking spoils, often violently, from Tidelander communities to make up for their losses.

A marginal note in confident, looping script: Peace, Penrose. Add to the record that many Tidelander lords felt perfectly justified in raiding the newcomers.

1100 – King Carlon dies. His son, Prince Harald, a fervent adherent of the Welded Church, takes the throne. On the coast, your niece Selida is born to Lord Valerian and Lady Frances Coralglass.

In confident, looping script: See my notes below.

1104 – King Harald, flush with the conquest and conversion of his eastern neighbors, invades the Tidelands in earnest. The Tideland princes unite to drive him back, but lose the Grand Temple of Aluna on the coast.

1105 – A son, Laurence, is born to Lord Valerian Coralglass. Tragically, Lady Frances passes in childbed.

1108 – The Dawnlanders press south along the coast. Lord Lydris Magnus, an ambitious Dawnlander architect, is gifted the ruins of the Grand Temple and the lands around it in recognition of his valor in battle. He elevates his squire, Garret Aegison, to knighthood.

1111 – Wyvernsvow Keep is completed. Fighting on the coast takes a tremendous toll on both sides. Prince Skyfawn's eldest son and heir is killed in battle, throwing the Tidelander alliance into jeopardy. Lord Magnus invites Prince Skyfawn, Lord (now General) Coralglass, and other Tidelander lords to Wyvernsvow for peace talks. Lord Coralglass brings his children: Selida, age eleven, and Laurence, age six. Prince Skyfawn brings his eldest daughter: Princess Emmeline, age sixteen.

1112 – The peace talks fail and war breaks out. Again.

1113 – On the other side of the continent, near the northern edge of the Dawnlands, Lord and Lady Whitepeak of Wintersend perish in an avalanche along with many of their retainers. The tragedy is blamed on the troll people from beyond the Dominion's border. As Kahldar, the Whitepeak heir, is only nine years old, his uncle is appointed regent and given authority over the province.

1115 – Prince Skyfawn dies in battle. Unable to rally the fracturing coastal lords alone, Princess Emmeline declares her marriage to Lord Lydris Magnus. Aluna's prohibition against making war on one's relatives prevents further immediate bloodshed. The Treaty of Wyvernsvow formalizes the peace and stipulates that, while the Tidelands will adopt the secular laws and taxes of the Dawnland Dominion, the Welded Church may not send priests or priestesses to preach or practice in the Tidelands. This preserves the independence of the Church of Aluna, instead of forcing Tidelanders to accept Aluna as a mere aspect of the Welded goddess Era. Dissidents, claiming the treaty is effectively a surrender, attempt to abduct Princess Emmeline via the caves under Wyvernsvow the night before the wedding. They fail.

In looping script: Call it what it is. We did surrender.

1116 — The new laws and taxes immediately impoverish the already-depleted treasuries of the Tidelander princes and lords, including Lord Coralglass and his heir, Laurence.

1117 — To encourage the Tidelands to accept Dominion rule and ameliorate widespread discontent with excessive taxation, King Harald creates a dowry purse against which Dawnlander lords can draw when offering for Tidelander brides. Lady Selida Coralglass receives an offer of marriage from a Dawnlander, but he withdraws his suit under mysterious circumstances. Lady Emmeline has the first of her three stillborn children.

1118 — Your predecessor, Grand Cleric Ethedra, formally accepts Lady Selida as a novitiate of the Church of Aluna.

1120 — Lord Valerian Coralglass attempts a rebellion. He is slain in combat, and King Harald takes possession of his lands. Laurence Coralglass is exiled and resorts to raiding along the coast. While competing with another privateer for a rich haul, his ship is lost with all hands.

1122 – Following her ordination, Lady Cleric Selida Coralglass begins to minister up and down the coast. Ser Kahldar Whitepeak, freshly knighted at eighteen, is sent by King Harald to help maintain order among the eastern peoples. Kahldar's uncle is officially made the new Lord of Wintersend.

1125 – The coastal peasants' revolt is decisively smothered. The penalty for minor secular infractions, such as theft and fisticuffs, is increased to public flogging and one year's hard labor.

1129 – Lord and Lady Magnus's prayers are answered with the birth of young Lydris almost fifteen years into their alliance. Lady Emmeline Magnus's deep gratitude to Aluna for this long-awaited blessing inspires a generous donation to the Church.

1130 – Stories begin to circulate regarding the Fox, an enigmatic folk hero of the coast who relieves Dawnlanders of their stolen treasure and frees wrongfully imprisoned Tidelanders.

1131 – Our cleric shortage grows more acute. Lady Selida's annual circuit is expanded to include Wyvernsvow Keep.

The same year, King Harald sends reinforcements to the Tidelands to aid in quelling unrest. Ser Kahldar White-peak, now twenty-seven, is among them.

1134 – Ser Kahldar is dispatched to Wyvernsvow in the spring and sworn to the service of the elder Lord Lydris Magnus. Lady Selida arrives at Wyvernsvow in time to lead the faithful in the Autumn Shoredance. Upon emerging triumphant in the harvest joust, Ser Kahldar bestows the victor's crown upon Lady Selida. In November, the elder Lord Lydris Magnus perishes in a hunting accident.

1135 – Exploring the caves under Wyvernsvow, young Lord Lydris discovers the lost cache of the former Grand Temple of Aluna. The Fox gathers a force to take it back.

Appended to the bottom, in confident, looping script: Penrose, I asked for an unbiased summary. Also, remove the personal elements. Your editorializing has been noted, but a good historian leaves no trace of their own intent in documents that may be discovered and misinterpreted later.

In careful script under that: A thousand pardons, Grand Cleric, but a good historian reveals what is relevant. A good politician leaves nothing that may be discovered and misinterpreted later.

A final note in confident, looping script: Thank you for your compliment, Penrose. Revision please.

APPENDIX B: CHARACTERS
DRAMATIS PERSONAE

Aluna: Tidemother; Goddess of the Sea, the Moon, and All Serpents. Worshipped in the Tidelands since time immemorial. Believed to have created everything in the world from snakes.

Exos: God of the Sun, originally worshipped in more orderly nations to the south. Though long opposed by the followers of Era, the Welded Church of the Heavens now venerates the two as husband and wife.

Era: Goddess of the Moon, traditionally worshipped by independent southern communities. Though historically a rival of Exos, the Welded Church of the Heavens now works to spread the good news of their holy union.

Exoeras: Deified prophet(s) whose teachings gave rise to the Welded Church of the Heavens. A priest and priestess—one dedicated to Exos and one to Era—who rose from the dead as a single individual after being martyred for Their forbidden love.

Selida Coralglass: An experienced cleric of Aluna. Travels the Tideland coast performing sacraments for her people.

Lord Valerian Coralgass: Her father, a Tidelander general. Slain in a failed rebellion against King Harald.

Laurence Coralglass: Her brother, a landless knight. Lost at sea after his exile.

The Grand Cleric of Aluna: The leader of her Church.

Lady Emmeline Magnus, née Princess Emmeline Skyfawn: Her childhood friend. Widow of the elder Lord Lydris Magnus. The Lady of Wyvernsvow Keep. Mother of young Lord Lydris. Ostensibly his regent.

Ser Kahldar Whitepeak: A chaste knight of the Dawnland Dominion. Practices the Welded faith. Stationed at Wyvernsvow for the past year and a half.

Young Lord Lydris Magnus: His six-year-old liege, to whom he owes fealty. Lord of Wyvernsvow Keep, and bright hope of the coast. Discovered a treasure under the castle this past summer.

Ser Garret Aegison: His commanding officer. Placed in charge of Wyvernsvow Keep by King Harald during Lady Emmeline Magnus's year of mourning.

Lord Lydris Magnus (Senior): His previous lord. Died in a hunting accident last year. Came to the Tidelands thirty-one years ago with the invading Dawnland army. Built Wyvernsvow Keep over the ruins of a destroyed temple of Aluna at the behest of King Harald. Married Princess (now Lady) Emmeline Skyfawn twenty years ago to secure peace on the coast.

Old Meg: Lady Emmeline's childhood nurse. Now young Lydris's nurse.

Dame Pottage: Wyvernsvow's cook.

The Fox: An outlaw who has been raiding Dawnlander lords up and down the coast. Now seeking young Lydris's treasure.

King Harald: The King of the Dawnland Dominion. In his late 50s. Instigated the invasion of the Tidelands when he came to power three decades ago. Considering converting all of his lands to the Welded religion upon his death.

ACKNOWLEDGMENTS

We offer heartfelt gratitude...

To cover artist Allie Strom, for propping her chin on her hand and asking what my "dream" was for the cover illustration. Thank you for being a good friend, for being the first person to read this story all the way through (twice!), for all your critical insights about the characters' believability and hauntedness, and, most of all, for coming to love Selida, Kahldar, and Emmeline like your own, and depicting them so stunningly. Serializing was scary, but your cover always reminded me that we were doing this together.

To our Author's Tea friends Angelo, Morgan, and Maya for reading endless versions of the first page. To Angelo for enunciating what Kahldar thought in modern speech, and for making me laugh out loud when you pointed out that Selida was using "thus" as an adverb. To Morgan for being the first person to encourage Selida in her conquest, for engaging deeply with the narrative, and for loving the story *for* its sparse depictions of emotion, instead of *in spite of* them.

To the Novel Writing Ladies: Cathy for "She can fix him, right" and "W H A T" and all your spot-on comments about motivation, characterization, and conflict. Victoria for your "cut all these paragraphs" and for reminding me that "the important thing is that [these characters are] fun to read." To Janelle for encouraging me to be unashamed of what I wrote and how it reflects my current values.

To Kevin, for encouraging me to be honest with myself and others about what this story was, and being the first person to tell me they loved it.

To Ginelle, for reading, discussing, and endorsing. For doing, like, ten NaNoWriMos to show us it's possible, and for sharing this writing dream with us.

To Brad, for understanding Kahldar's chivalry.

To Max, for reading a draft far outside your genre, and reminding me how lucky we've both been. It's true. We are.

To Geetika and Deren, for your novel marketing ideas.

To Kate, for finishing the draft at 6:00am before our call so you could give me feedback face to face.

To Aaron, who wanted to be in a book I wrote. The pressure! To clarify, lest there be any doubt: You are the heroic squire, not the dastardly minstrel.

To Tom, for encouraging me to visualize what the end of this writing career could be.

To Ann, for pointing out that most of my exposition problems could be solved with a map and a list of dramatis personae, both of which became the most-viewed chapters of the story during its serialization.

To Gin, for reading every chapter, commenting on Royal Road, and teaching me the ropes of that wonderful place.

To Gladiolus, for creating and nurturing your Write and Bitch Discord, and being such good company on this self publishing journey. To HappyQuill for your advice on Wattpad, and to Quips for putting up that Reddit post about how much you wanted a stoic, chaste knight.

To Andrew, again, for the campaign that inspired this story, these characters, and this conflict. Also, for D&D, where Rodrigo and I regularly return to become the best versions of ourselves. Also: To David for hauling Selida back up onto the roof five minutes into the session after she rolled that 1 and was totally going to fall to her death in the courtyard.

To Mami and Papi, for raising voracious readers and encouraging us in this new career.

To Aubrey, Willy, Lily, and Avery for giving us such hope for the future.

To Mommy and Daddy, who let me read whatever and whenever I wanted, so all the flowers of human history could be my friends and teachers.

And finally: To everyone who encouraged, helped, and gave us the space to give our very best to this story, including you, reading this right now. *All the Serpents in the Sky*, like many first books, is oddly cross-genre, a little lumpy in its pacing, and definitely overstuffed. Our hope has always been that it will find its way to the twenty people on the planet for whom it is exactly built. Thank you for coming on this journey with us, and please stay in touch.

– S. R. Dreamholde, January 2026

About the Author(s)

Stephanie and Rodrigo first met when they were fourteen, and fell in love soon thereafter. Now they write and edit from their nest of old books and gem-hued electronics.

When they're not working on a romance novel or editing a new sourcebook, they play video games and tabletop RPGs. Cookies, plushies, and good stories make them happy.

www.dreamholde.com